Unraveling Rage

A.G. Hailstalk

For Mom and Dad....I love you.

Dear Reader,

I have contemplated whether or not I should publish this novel due to its painful subject matter. However, as a writer, once you have an idea, it's hard to not stop thinking about it until you put it on a page.

After thinking about the pros and cons of putting this story out there for everyone to read, I've decided to publish it. I feel like for all the progress we've made as a country, we are taking steps back to a time when places in this country were separate but not equal.

Having relatives who grew up in the Jim Crow South I know just how bad things can get when people hate; what hate can make someone capable of.

In addition to having to go to a really dark place to write this, the n-word, sexism, homophobic, anti-Semitic, and other bigoted terms are used in this novel in order for me to write a story about bigotry and hatred as authentically and honestly as possible.

With everything being said, I hope this story pulls you in and never wants to let you go until the very last page.

Sincerely,
A.G. Hailstalk

Ch. 1

With curlers in her hair, Abby Block puts on her little black dress with silver high heel shoes. She walks over to her vanity and puts on her makeup. Abby is meeting her parents, Mark and Betty Block, for dinner to celebrate her acceptance into Charm Vault Pharmaceuticals' Human Resources Leadership Development Program in her hometown of Still Vo, New Jersey. Her apartment complex just happens to be in Still Vo too. It has a doorman on duty 24/7, a full-size gym, an outdoor pool and hot tub, and conference rooms. Abby's sizeable apartment has two bedrooms. She has a full size kitchen with a granite countertop. Next to the kitchen is a table with four chairs and a living room with a flat screen TV. It also has a washer and dryer unit.

Tomorrow is her first day of work and she is so excited.

Wow! I can't wait for my first day tomorrow! All of those all-nighters during Tumble Top University's HR grad program paid off! I can officially call myself a working professional! On top of that, my BFF, Kate Winger, will be joining me in the HR program too! Yay!

Abby takes her rollers out and rakes her fingers through her beautiful long, hair. She hears her phone ring and sees Betty on the caller ID. She picks up:

"Hi Mom! I'm about to walk out in 20 seconds. I'll be at the restaurant in a few."

"Okay sweetie! See you soon! I love you!"

"I love you too!"

She leaves her apartment and shuts her door.

Mark, Betty, and Abby are at the table enjoying their dinner at the Pasta Lava, their favorite Italian Restaurant in Still Vo. Mark is in his blue button up shirt with black pants and Betty is in her beautiful royal blue dress. Abby is having pasta with meatballs, Betty is having Fettuccini Alfredo, and Mark is having Ravioli. Mark holds up his glass of champagne and says, "To our wonderful, successful daughter who has made us so proud!"

Betty and Abby hold up their champagne and clink their glasses with Mark's. Betty jumps in, "Very proud indeed!"

"Thanks Mom and Dad!"

Betty says, "So how does this program work again?"

"So I get to work in all of the sub departments of the HR department. After the program, I get to decide which sub department I want to be in, of course that depends on Charm Vault's business needs. OMG I'm so excited about orientation tomorrow! I get to meet all of the other HRLDP participants! It's so exciting!!!!!! I can't wait!!!!!"

Mark says, "I don't know why you were so worried about landing a full-time job after school! I knew you could do it!"

"But I couldn't have done it without you and Mom!"

Betty says, "Honey, you did *all* of the work!"

"But if it wasn't for your moral support, I probably wouldn't have gotten here! I can't thank the two of you enough for that!"

Betty reaches over to kiss Abby on the cheek, "Sweetie, we have a surprise for you!"

Abby hears people sing happy birthday. She turns around and sees several waiters and waitresses walk over to her table with a chocolate cake and a candle on top. The cake is put down and after the singing stops, Abby closes her eyes, makes a wish, and blows out the candle. Everyone claps and leaves the table. The Blocks dig their forks into the cake and take a bite.

"Mom.....Dad.....my birthday is not until tomorrow."

Betty says, "We know sweetie! But we're at your favorite restaurant so why not? By the way, there is going to be a huge surprise for you tomorrow!!"

"A surprise?! For me?! What is it!?"

"Abby.....it's a surprise for a reason! I can't tell you!"

"Oh Mom!"

The waiter comes over with the check, "Here you go!"

Mark puts his credit card in the black book and gives it back to the waiter, "We're all set Mr."

The waiter thanks him and walks off.

"Dad.......I could've paid for my part!"

"Honey, you haven't started your new job yet and by the way, you're getting the tab next time!"

"Oh Dad!"

The Blocks get up from the table and start heading out. When they're outside, Abby gives a big hug to Betty:

"I love you very much Mom!"

"I love you too sweetie!"

Then she gives Mark a big hug:

"I love you very much Dad!"

"I love you too honey!"

"Abby, text me when you get home."

"Mom."

"Abby?"

"Okay......I will. See you two tomorrow!"

Betty said, "See you Abby!"

Mark said, "Bye!"

Ch. 2

Betty and Mark pull up in their driveway and enter their beautiful mansion in Lavish Valley, the richest part of the affluent town of Still Vo. Their home is white with a double porch that wraps all the way around the house. It has 6 bedrooms and 6 1/2 bathrooms, if you count the powder room in the foyer. The kitchen has a granite countertop and an island. The living room has a large L-shaped black leather couch and a large flat screen TV on the wall. The dining room is large with a gorgeous chandelier hanging in the center of the room. The backyard is incredible. It has a huge pool with a waterfall and a hot tub. There is a sizable pool house behind it that has two bedrooms, 2 1/2 bathrooms, if you count the powder room on the first floor, and a full size kitchen and living room with a television. Next to the pool section is a beautiful English garden and a gazebo in the center of it.

Now don't let their advantages fool you. Mark and Betty are not privileged. Both of them grew up in working class families in New Jersey and are the first in their families to graduate from college. This black couple worked themselves to the bone to earn all of this. Entrepreneurs Mark and Betty founded one of top marketing firms in New York City. They sold the business for a hell of a lot of money and they are now part-time business instructors at Tumble Top University in New Jersey. Yes, that's the school Abby went to. Abby did not want to pursue a career in marketing. She really liked her Intro to Human Resources class and the rest was history.

Abby is very privileged you see. But Mark and Betty did not want to raise a spoiled daughter. Her parents wanted her to realize that nice things don't just show up. They told her, "You have to be twice as good as every white person you work with at the office just to get the same amount of credit as they do. Yes it's unfair but it's the way things are and if you want to be as successful as your mom and dad, then you're going to have to play that game and stay two steps ahead."

Betty and Mark enter into the kitchen and are greeted by their gray colored Akita dog, Lala. They pet her and walk upstairs to their master bedroom. Lala follows them. It has a huge king size bed with a seating area next to it with a light blue small L-shaped couch and chairs and a small table. It has a big bathroom attached to it with a jacuzzi tub and shower. It has two sinks built into a marble countertop. The walls are painted light blue in the bedroom and bathroom.

Lala sits on her bed. Betty takes her phone out of her purse.

"Let me see if Abby text me yet."

"Honey, Abby's 23 years old. She'll be 24 tomorrow. I'm sure she's fine."

"Well just because you think she's fine doesn't mean I feel the same way."

Betty breathes a sigh of relief when she sees Abby's text: *Hi Mom! I'm home! Love you!*

"See? She's fine!"

Betty shot a look at Mark.

"Don't give me that look!"

"I know she's grown! But no matter how old she is, Abby will always be my baby. After all, she's my only baby! You hear me?"

"Yes ma'am!," Mark said jokingly.

Betty rolled her eyes, "Oh Mark! Anyway, I'm going to bed. Love you."

Betty and Mark kiss each other and get ready for bed.

Ch. 3

Kate Winger and Abby Block have been friends for almost 20 years. She grew up on the same block as Abby in Lavish Valley. They also attended the same HR masters program. Kate's parents, Andrew and Allie, both grew up in working-class families in Virginia. Both of them are the first in their families to graduate from college. They founded a luxury retail company in New York City. They sold it for a hell a lot of money and her parents are now part-time instructors at Tumble Top University. Kate's parents are also great friends with Abby's parents.

It's Kate's first day as an HRLDP associate at Charm Vault. She's the first one in the conference room for orientation. Her red hair is flat ironed and she is wearing a pastel pink dress with matching shoes.

Wow. This is weird. Abby would've been here by now.

She calls Abby.....it rang and went to voicemail.

She tries to reach her a few more times. No success.

Tammie Trolly, the daughter of Tom Trolly, President and Chief Executive Officer of Charm Vault, walks into the room. She's also an associate of the HR program.

Tammie grew up in Broomville, New Jersey, an affluent town right next to Still Vo. Her great-grandparents founded Charm Vault. Her uncle, Keith Trolly is the Chief Financial Officer of the company.

She flips her long blond hair back as she sits down in her orange dress and blazer.

"Hi Kate."

"Hi Tammie."

"Kate....nice dress! It would've been nicer if it was a little more formal."

"So funny you say that. The email we received specifically said to dress business casual. So...it would've been nice if you've followed directions."

"Oh honey! I'm just trying to help."

"Really? Because the last time I checked, helpfulness doesn't come in sour packages....honey."

Tammie forms a grimace look on her face. While Kate simply smiles.

Kate returns to her phone texting Abby trying to get a hold of her.

Hey Abby! WHERE THE HELL ARE YOU?! Orientation is about to start!!! You're worrying me!!!! Give me a call as soon as you get this!

"Kate...um shouldn't you put your phone away?"

"Sour packages......Tammie?"

Tammie rolled her eyes.

Two ladies walked in showcasing their long brunette hair and blue eyes. Their names are Gabby Fry and Fiona Pipe. Gabby is wearing a blue dress and blazer with black heels. Fiona is wearing a green dress and blazer with black heels. The girls are Tammie's friends.

Tammie says, "Hey girls! Love your outfits!"

Gabby and Fiona said, "Thanks!"

Tammie then turns to Kate and continues talking.

"You see what happens when you listen to me.....Kate?"

Kate chuckles, "Yeah! If I'd listened to you, I would look colorfully ridiculous!"

The three ladies just looked at her.

Three white ladies and gentlemen who are program participants, entered the room in business casual attire.

A white woman, Eve Wonder, the Director of the HR Leadership Development Program of Charm Vault, enters the room.

"Good Morning Everyone! I'm glad all of you are here!"

She looks at Tammie, Gabby, and Fiona.

"Um ladies.....you only had to dress business casual."

Tammie said, "Yeah....but there's no such thing as being too dressed up right Eve?"

"Well when you're part of a team Tammie......yeah there is such a thing."

Tammie gives Eve a look.

Eve continues talking to the group.

"So we'll get started in a little bit."

Eve sees a middle-aged white woman, Danielle Sharp, Chief Human Resources Officer of Charm Vault, enter the room."

"Hello Everyone!"

"Hello Danielle," everyone says in unison.

"I'm so happy to see all of you! I'm sure Eve can take it from here."

She turns to Eve.

"So sorry to interrupt but I need to borrow Kate for a bit."

"Of course Danielle."

Kate and Danielle leave the room and enter Danielle's office, which looks like any other C-suite, except it's in Tiffany blue with a soft, gray carpet.

Danielle sits on her light blue couch and pulls her brunette hair up in a ponytail.

"Kate, please sit."

Kate sits next to Danielle on the couch.

"Kate, where is Abby? Is she okay? She should be here by now! Is she sick or something?"

"Danielle......I'm asking the same question you are. I spoke to her early yesterday morning on the phone. She sounded so excited and everything! She didn't seem sick to me! I have no idea where she is! I tried calling and texting her multiple times and she's not picking up!"

Danielle tries to reach Abby on her cell phone......no answer.

"Hi Abby. This is Danielle! Where are you? Orientation is about to start! Please call me as soon as you get this message. Hope everything is okay. Bye."

Danielle hangs up and retrieves Abby's application. She starts dialing another number........Betty's number.

Betty is in her pajamas having coffee on her porch outside reading the newspaper when she hears her cell phone ringing.

"Hello?"

"Betty? Betty this is Danielle-"

"Oh hi Danielle! How are you?"

"Betty, Abby's not here! Do you have any idea where she is?"

"Abby's not there?!"

"No!"

"Isn't this her first day?"

"Yeah! Orientation is about to start in a few minutes! I've tried reaching her and she's not picking up!"

Betty's newspaper slips out of her hands and she starts trembling.

"WHAT?! Danielle……Danielle……let me reach her….hold on."

Betty reaches Abby several times and leaves a message.

"Abby?! Where are you?! Are you okay?! You're supposed to be at work!!! Call me when you get this ASAP! You're scaring me!"

Betty goes back to Danielle.

"Danielle….I can't reach her! I'm going over to her apartment! This is not like her!"

"I know Betty! Call me when you get there!"

"Bye!"

Betty hangs up and runs upstairs to her bedroom. She runs up to Mark, who's still in bed. She shakes him.

"Mark! Mark! MARK! Wake up!"

Mark is groggy and looks annoyed.

"Betty-"

"Wake up damn it!"

"Why?!"

"Abby's missing!!! She didn't show up for work this morning!!!"

Mark jumps out of bed.

"WHAT?! Where the hell is she?!"

"I don't know but I'm going over to her place right now!"

Betty grabs her purse while Mark slips on his robe. They run downstairs and get into their black Audi and speed off.

––––––––––

They arrive at Abby's apartment building. The doorman, Gary, sees the couple walking up.

"Betty! Mark! Is everything okay? I was just about to call you! My nightshift guy told me that he didn't see Abby come home last night!"

Betty's eyes widen, "WHAT?!"

Mark asks, "Are you *sure* he didn't see Abby come in last night or early this morning?!"

"Mark, he is 100% sure. We would check the security cameras but……..they're still broken."

"Mark let's go!"

"Go where Betty?!"

"To Abby's room!"

"Betty! Didn't you hear what Gary just said?!"

"I don't give a damn what Gary says I'm going to my daughter's room to look for her! So are you coming or not?!"

Mark takes a deep breath, "Okay."

The couple hops on the elevator to the 8th floor where Abby's apartment is. Betty's hand shakes as she tries to put her key in the doorknob.

"Honey......want me to get it?"

"NO!"

They both enter. Betty starts screaming and Mark walks through the unit.

"ABBY?!"

No answer.

"ABBY?! WHERE THE HELL ARE YOU?!"

No answer.

"ABBY ANSWER ME!!!"

No answer.

"PLEASE HONEY! WHERE ARE YOU?!"

Mark comes back to Betty, "I've looked everywhere Betty.........no sign of her."

"Goddammit Mark! That's because you didn't look hard enough!"

Betty starts walking around the unit.

"ABBY?! ABBY?! ABBY?! ABBYYYYYYYYYYYYYYYYYYYYYYYYYY?!"

Betty returns back to the entrance way and collapses on the floor to her knees. She is in a daze.

"Mark......Mark.......where the HELL IS MY BABY?! WHERE THE HELL IS MY BABY GIRL?! WHERE THE HELL IS MY DAUGHTER?!"

Betty starts bawling and starts pounding her fists on the floor.

"WHERE IS SHE!? WHERE IS SHE MARK?!"

Mark stands there in a daze.

"SHIT MARK! ANSWER ME!!!! FUCKING ANSWER ME!!!!!!"

"SHIT BETTY! WHAT THE FUCK DO YOU WANT ME TO DO?! HUH?! WHAT KIND OF FUCKING ANSWER DO I HAVE FOR THAT?! HUH?!"

Mark collapses on the floor with Betty and starts crying. He reaches over to hug her.

After Betty catches her breath, she says, "I have to call Danielle back.....tell her that Abby's not here."

Betty reaches for her phone.

Ch. 5

"Betty?! Did you find her?!"

"No! She's gone Danielle! Damn it she's not here!"

"WHAT?!"

Kate hears what's going on.

"Danielle! Abby's not home?!"

"No......no she's not Kate..."

"Let me speak to her Danielle!"

"Kate-"

"I want to speak to her. Now! Please!"

Danielle hands her the phone.

"Aunt Betty......Aunt Betty it's Kate!"

"KATE!!!!!!! Oh God oh God oh God!!!! I can't find her! She's gone!!!!!!!"

Kate tries to hold back her tears.

"I know.....I know.....um.....I'll be over there in a few okay?!"

"Oh Kate! Don't! It's your first day!"

"Yeah.....I don't care about that, okay?! See you in a little bit! Love you!"

Kate hangs up the phone.

"Danielle, I'll just use a personal day."

"Kate......don't worry about that.....okay?"

"Okay thanks."

Kate exited the building and dashes towards her car. When she gets in, she bawls her eyes out.

Where is Abby?! Where is she?! What if someone has done something bad to her and there's nothing I could've done to save her?!

Once Kate catches her breath, she starts her silver Land Rover. All of the sudden, Fiona appears in Kate's window. Kate jumps and rolls down her window.

"Kate……I……didn't mean to scare you. Uh……where are you going? Orientation-"

"FUCK ORIENTATION FIONA!!! ABBY IS MISSING!!!"

"WHAT?! That can't be! I mean…….she must have overslept or something!"

"Her parents went to her apartment…….she's not there."

"Well……I'm sure she'll turn up somewhere……right?"

Kate's eyes well up again.

"I don't know Fiona…..I don't know. Look…I have to go alright?"

"Well good luck. Give my regards to her parents….okay?"

"Okay Fiona."

Fiona puts her hand on Kate's shoulder.

"Kate."

"What?"

"I'm………sorry."

"Thanks."

As Fiona walks away, Kate rolls up the window and speeds out of the parking lot.

Wow…….so that bitch Fiona has a heart after all.

Ch. 6

Allie is sitting at the kitchen table in her large mansion reading a book and having coffee when her cell phone rings. It's Betty.

"Hey Betty! How are you?"

"ALLIE! ABBY'S MISSING!!!!"

"WHAT?! THAT CAN'T BE!"

"I'm in her apartment right now and she's not here!"

"Well......well......Betty......did you call her boyfriend, Evan?"

"Allie, there's no way she's with Evan! He's on a business trip in London."

Betty suddenly realizes something.

"Oh God! Allie!"

"What? What's wrong?"

"Evan.......he's coming back this afternoon! Oh God! How the fuck am I going to tell him Allie?!"

"Betty......Betty......I'll be there in a few minutes okay? See you soon."

"Okay Allie........"

Allie hangs up the phone and runs up her grand stairwell into her master bedroom. She wakes up Andrew, who is still asleep.

"Andrew!!! Andrew!!! Andrew wake the hell up!"

Andrew is very groggy as he turns over to Allie.

"What Allie?!"

"Abby's missing!"

Andrew swings out of bed.

"What?!"

Allie's eyes start to well up.

"She's been missing all morning Andrew! That sweet girl is gone!"

Allie gets up and puts her robe on. She puts her long, red hair in a ponytail.

"Allie….where are you going?"

"Betty needs me!"

Andrew puts his robe on.

"I'm coming with you!"

They hop into their black Mercedes sports car and speed off.

Ch. 7

A middle-aged white male police officer arrives at Abby's apartment.

"So......what exactly happened here?"

Betty gives him a look.

"Uh.....my daughter is missing!!! Can't you see that?"

"And.......when was the last time you saw her?"

"My husband and I saw her last night. We were having dinner."

"Where?"

"At Pasta Lava."

"Okay...."

"Okay what?," says Betty.

"Look ma'am. Your daughter is an adult okay? Are you sure she's not off with some guy or whatever?"

Mark stood up, "What exactly do you mean officer?"

"Well........young woman missing without a trace. Most likely, she ran off with a guy that y'all didn't approve of. After all, young women tend to do that anyway."

Betty gives him a glaring look.

"She has a boyfriend! So no! She didn't run off with some *guy!*"

The officer chuckles, "Are you sure ma'am?"

Betty gives him another glaring look.

"Are you *sure* you know what you're doing? Or do you just not care?"

A young black woman and a young white woman in black pantsuits enter the apartment.

The black woman starts to speak, "Hi Mr. and Mrs. Block. My name is Detective Jackie Barns and this is my partner Detective Heidi Smith. We're very sorry about your daughter, Abby."

Betty responds, "Thank you."

She looks at the officer and keeps talking.

"At least somebody gives a shit."

Betty slightly shakes her head.

"Uh.........sorry........Detective Barns and Detective Smith. My mind has been.........a little out of sorts.

Heidi says, "It's okay Mrs. Block. No worries."

Jackie says, "So I know this is tough for both of you but we need you to answer some questions, okay?"

Mark and Betty nod.

Jackie continues, "Okay. So when was the last time you two saw Abby?"

The officer interjects, "Oh.....they saw her at the Pasta Lava for dinner yesterday...yeah."

Jackie and Heidi give him a look.

Jackie says, "Uh...let Mr. and Mrs. Block answer my questions. Got it?"

"Look I already asked them that question. There's no sense in going back to it again."

"And there's no sense in how lightly you're taking this situation....Officer Charles Bark."

Charles chuckles, "I am taking this seriously."

Heidi jumps in, "Really? Because the last time I checked, nobody *chuckles* when they're taking something seriously."

Charles forms a shocked look on his face.

Betty responds, "My husband and I saw her last night. We were all having dinner at the Pasta Lava."

"Okay. What time did you and your husband come home from dinner?"

"At around 9PM."

"Did you ever get in contact with Abby after dinner?"

"Yes. She texted me letting me know that she got home. Oh I have the text if you want to see it."

"Yes please. That will be helpful."

Betty finds the text on her phone and gives it to Jackie.

"Okay. So she texted you at around 9:15PM that she arrived home."

"Heidi asked, "Do you mind if I take a look around?"

Mark responded, "No. Go ahead."

Heidi starts walking around the apartment while Jackie continues to ask questions.

"And you haven't heard from her since this last text?"

Betty replied, "No."

Heidi looks at pictures of Abby with her family and friends. Then she spots a picture of her with Evan.

She asks, "Mr. and Mrs. Block, does Abby have a boyfriend?"

Mark replies, "Yes. His name is Evan Pale. He's a software engineer."

"How long have they been together?"

"Five years."

"Is this Evan right here Mr. Block?"

Mark walks over to the picture Heidi is pointing at.

"Yes Detective Smith. That's him."

"Do you know anything about his whereabouts?"

Betty jumps in, "He's in London for business. His flight is expected to arrive here this afternoon."

"Mrs. Block, do you know what time?"

"Around 4PM."

Jackie jumps in, "We'll need to question him at some point when he gets back."

"And her friends at some point too," said Heidi.

Betty looks at both of the detectives, "Why....are you asking to speak with her boyfriend and friends?"

Heidi replies, "We have to rule everyone out close to Abby. Standard procedure."

Jackie says, "It's nothing personal."

Betty's eyes start to well up.

"None of them would hurt a hair on Abby's head! None of them would do this! Please find the person who did this to my daughter, please!"

Jackie put her hand on Betty's shoulder, "Mrs. Block-"

"Please call me Betty!"

"Betty....we'll do everything we can to find your daughter. But we have to follow standard procedure to cover all of our basis, okay?"

Heidi walks over to Betty and takes her hand, "It's okay."

"Detective Smith-"

"You can call me Heidi. It's fine."

"And you can call me Jackie."

"Heidi.....Jackie.....do you have kids?"

Betty shakes her head.

"Sorry.....that was a personal question. I shouldn't have..."

Jackie says, "No no.....it's perfectly fine for you to ask that. My wife and I have a son and daughter."

Heidi says, "My husband and I have a daughter. So yeah......we know exactly how you feel and we will do everything to find her.....okay?"

"Okay."

Mark jumps in, "Betty, let the detectives do their job. They seem to really care about this...okay?"

Holding back tears, Betty says, "Okay."

Switching the subject, Heidi asks, "Betty...does Abby have a car?"

"Yes."

"What kind?"

"A dark blue Land Rover."

"Oh...all of the attendants here have an assigned parking space," says Mark.

Heidi says, "That's very helpful! Let's go down to see if her car is there!"

The detectives, The Blocks, and Officer Charles, head to the parking lot.

"What her parking space number?," asks Jackie.

Betty says, "It's number 33."

They arrive at parking spot number 33.........Abby's car is nowhere in sight.

Mark puts his hands on his head, "Oh no! Oh God!"

Betty reaches into her bag, "Wait....I have an extra key fob in here to her car!"

Betty presses the alarm button......no sound. She presses it again......still no sound.

Jackie notices Heidi's eyes are widening as she moves closer to the empty parking space........there is a sizable pool of blood to the left of the space.

"Holy shit Jackie. This.......isn't looking good."

"Oh shit.....Heidi I'll call our boss about this."

"I'll call CSU over here....."

Mark and Betty see what's going on with Jackie and Heidi. They run towards them.

They see the pool of blood and run faster screaming. But Jackie and Heidi block them from getting close to it.

Jackie says, "Sorry Mark and Betty. We can't let you go near this."

Heidi says, "Sorry you two. We can't.."

Betty starts to wail, "WHAAAAAAAT HAPPENED TO MY BABY?!?!?!?! AHHHHHHHHH!!!!!"

Marks starts wailing, "WHY HER GOD?!?!? WH- WHY HER?!?!?!"

Ch. 8

Andrew, Allie, and Kate find a parking space in the parking lot of Abby's building and get out of their cars. Allie sees Kate.

"KATE!!!!"

Kate turns to her mother and runs to her for a hug.

"MOM!!!"

They both start crying.

"Mom, did you hear what happened?!"

"Yes sweetie!"

Andrew walks over and put his arms around both of them. All of the sudden they hear people wailing. Kate moves away from her parents.

"Mom....Dad.....do you hear that?"

Allie replies, "Yeah....."

Andrew points to the direction where it's coming from, "It sounds like it's up there!"

"Andrew.....honey........I think I know who's crying......"

The three of them run towards the sound. They find out who it is. Betty and Mark are on the asphalt bawling their eyes out. Betty looks up and sees The Wingers. She steadily gets up and runs to Allie, almost knocking her down with her powerful hug.

"AAAAALLLLLLLLIIIIEEEEE!!!!!!!!!"

Allie whispers into Betty's ear, "Betty.........is that......blood in Abby's parking space?"

Betty nods her head.

Allie starts to tremble.

Andrew walks over to Mark and helps him up. The second Mark is on his feet, he aggressively hugs Andrew and continues crying.

Kate stands there in shock. Heidi walks over to her while Jackie tries keeps the others calm.

"You must be one of Abby's friends."

"Excuse me?"

"Oh....I'm sorry....I'm Detective Heidi Smith. I had a chance to walk through your friend's apartment and saw you in some of the pictures she had. What's your name?"

"Kate......Kate Winger."

"And I'm assuming those are your parents over there with your parents."

"Yes.....Andrew and Allie Winger. Um.........Detective?"

"Yes?"

Kate's arm trembles as she raises it to point to the pool of blood.

"Is........that.........blood in Abby's parking spot?"

Heidi hesitates for a few seconds.

"Yes.......I'm afraid so."

Kate stares at the blood.

"Kate? Would you like to sit down for a few?"

Kate just looks at Heidi and faints.

Heidi catches her, "Kate.....Kate.....oh no."

Allie sees her daughter, "KATE! KATE!"

She runs over to her.

"KATE! KATE! Kate it's Mom! Wake up! Wake up! Sweetie, c'mon! Please!"

Kate comes out of her fainting spell.

Andrew says, "I'll get some water from the car."

Heidi says, "Deep breathes Kate, deep breathes. There you go."

Jackie looks around for Officer Charles.

"Uh…..has anyone seen Officer Charles anywhere?"

Heidi turns her head, "No….no I haven't seen him anywhere."

Jackie whispers to herself, "Asshole."

Jackie sees CSU arrive at the scene.

"Heidi…we need to get all of them out of here. I see the CSU truck arriving."

Heidi turns to The Blocks and The Wingers.

"Okay everyone. CSU has arrived. We need all of you to clear the scene okay?"

Allie looks at Betty, "Betty……we need to leave so that the police can find out who took Abby…okay?"

"But Allie-"

"Betty…..let's go to your house. You need to rest after today….okay?"

When Betty finally agrees, everyone starts leaving the scene.

Betty called out, "Wait! Jackie……Heidi…..there's something I need to tell you."

Jackie looks at Heidi, "Yeah Betty. What is it?"

"Today……..is Abby's birthday……she turns 24…."

Jackie looks at Heidi again, "Wow…..um…….I'm sorry to hear that Betty."

Heidi responds, "Me too."

Allie gently brings Betty along with her, "C'mon Betty."

When the families are out of ear shot, Jackie says to Heidi, "And I thought this day couldn't get any worse for them…."

Heidi responds, "Lets just hope that Abby's birthday isn't also her death day."

A few minutes later, CSU begins taking photos of the parking spot.

Jackie states, "That parking spot and the victim's apartment needs to be analyzed."

Heidi states, "From top to bottom."

Ch. 9

The Blocks and The Wingers arrive at Betty and Mark's mansion. Betty slowly walks to the kitchen island and plops on the stool.

Allie walks to the wine rack, "I'll get the cabernet out."

Kate grabs the Jack Daniels and makes jack on the rocks. Allie notices what she is pouring.

"Sweetie....do you want that mixed in with anything?"

"No."

"Kate now-"

"Mom! My best friend is missing! I don't know if she's even alive at this point!"

"Kate don't you *dare* say that!"

Tears well up in Kate eyes.

"Did you see that pool of blood Mom?! Did you?! There was *a lot* of it..."

Allie's eyes start to well up. Kate swishes her drink around and tears begin to roll down her cheeks.

"Now if you would excuse me.........I'm going have this drink that will help me not feel a damn thing.......because right now.......I really hate how I'm feeling......"

"Kate-"

Kate walks away with her drink....and the bottle.

Allie takes a deep breath, opens the cabernet, and pours two glasses. Andrew goes into the fridge and grabs a six-pack of beer.

"Andrew......why in the hell do you need a whole damn six pack of that?"

"It's not for me Allie."

Andrew tilts his head over to Mark, who's just sitting on the living room couch in a daze.

"Now if you would excuse me, I need to make sure this man doesn't fall apart more than he already has."

Andrew walks away.

Allie walks towards Betty with the glasses.....and the bottle.

"Here you go Betty."

"Thanks...."

Betty and Allie take big sips of their wine.

Allie begins to cry.

Betty.......is it really........Abby's birthday today?"

Betty begins to cry.

"Yeah......."

Allie puts her hand on Betty's back.

"Did you have anything planned for her?"

"No...but Evan did....he wouldn't tell us what is was."

Lala walks up to Betty and she starts petting her.

Andrew gives a beer to Mark.

"Thanks."

Mark and Andrew open their beers and take a big sip.

So it's really Abby's birthday today?"

"Yeah didn't you just hear man?!"

Mark shakes his head.

"Sorry man it's just...."

Marks begins to cry.

Andrew pats Mark's back, "It's okay man. Don't worry about it."

Ch. 10

Kate walks upstairs to Abby's room. It's painted in lavender. It has a full sized bed and a flat screen TV across from it mounted on the wall. Next to it is a seating area with two purple plush chairs and couch. It has it's own bathroom with a Jacuzzi tub and separate shower. It has a marble countertop where the sink is. It is also painted in lavender.

She takes a big sip of her whiskey, sits on the couch and puts her drink and the bottle on the coffee table. A flashback comes to her.

————

Abby and Kate are on their way back from dinner during their second semester of graduate school. They pass a lecture hall and see a familiar face in the window.

"Oh my God Kate.....is that....."

"Danielle Sharp, Chief Human Resources Officer of Charm Vault Pharmaceuticals?!"

"Holy......."

"Shit! She's here! She's here at Tumble Top!"

"Holy.....shit!"

"Damn right!"

Abby walks towards the door.

"Abby......what the *hell* are you doing?"

"Walking in of course! I wanna find out what the woman has to say!"

"What?"

"Oh c'mon Kate! After all, there's no do not enter sign on the door!"

"Well.........okay!"

Both girls enter the lecture hall and take a seat in the back. The overhead projector says *Welcome Guest Lecturer Danielle Sharp, Chief Human Resources Officer at Charm Vault Pharmaceuticals.* Danielle keeps talking.

"So Human Resources back in the day was known as an administrative function. HR was known for keeping track of personnel files, dealing with employee discipline, and things of that nature. Now, HR is being looked at as a more strategic function because companies are looking at them as the professionals who are managing their most important asset, their employees. So now more organizations are depending on HR to figure out where the best talent is, how to retain the company's high performing employees, and things of that nature. The HR profession is changing and in order for a company to stay competitive......and recruit and retain top talent, they need to start realizing that HR is being looked at as a strategic function...and not just an administrative one. Right now, I'm trying to get Charm Vault to see my department as such."

The professor moves to the front of the room, "Thank you Ms. Sharp for coming today! We've learned so much!"

Everyone stands up and applauses.

"Ms. Sharp, do you have time to answer questions?"

"Of course I do!"

A couple of people raised their hands and asked Danielle some questions.

Then Abby raises her hand. Kate leans over to her.

"Abby....what are you doing?"

Abby doesn't answer.

Danielle spots Abby.

"Um......you."

"Ms. Sharp! First of all, thank you so much for coming to our school to speak with us today."

"You're welcome."

"Ms. Sharp, I know that you just started the CHRO role at Charm Vault a few months ago but it seems like you're making some major changes already. Have you considered implementing a Human Resources Leadership Development Program for the company?"

"I have........considered it. But because things have been very busy, it's been put on the back burner for now."

"How about my friend Kate and I help you with that?"

"Kate?"

Kate gives Abby a wide-eyed look and then raises her hand.

"Hi Ms. Sharp! Nice to meet you!"

"Why...........don't you ladies come down here afterwards and discuss this, okay?"

Abby and Kate look at each other.

"Okay!"

After the session is over, the girls walk over to Danielle.

They both said, "Hi Ms. Sharp!"

"Hi ladies! I know Professor Hugh is a biggie on formality but........you can just call me Danielle!"

They all laugh. Then Danielle continues.

"So have you ladies landed an internship yet?"

They look at each other, look at her, and said, "No......not yet."

"Let's see......today is Monday right?"

They nod.

"We're currently looking for some HR Interns this summer......you ladies are currently students right?"

Abby says, "Yes! We're both in the HR masters program!"

Kate says, "We're graduating next year!"

"Even better! Are both of you free on Friday?"

They nod.

"Great!"

Kate says, "Both of us have business cards if you would like our information."

"Wow! You ladies are always prepared! Very impressive! Yes I would love both of your cards."

They give her their cards.

Danielle then reaches in her bag.

"Here is my card. Please send me your resumes. I will gives these cards to my executive assistant so she will email you what time you two should be at the office on Friday for your interview for the HR Internship program. Sound good?"

They nod.

"Great! See you ladies on Friday! Have a great day!"

They both said, "You too!"

As they leave the lecture hall, Professor Hugh calls them out.

"I don't remember you ladies being in my class!"

They turn around slowly to face him.

"You know…I'm teaching an organizational development class next semester. If you're interested, I highly encourage you two to sign up."

Kate answers, "Thanks Professor for the invitation but we're in the HR grad program."

"Even better ladies! I'm teaching a class in the grad program next semester called HR and Finance and I've been able to arrange the entire class to visit the New York Stock Exchange! I encourage you ladies to register for it!"

Abby said, "Well thank you Professor Hugh!"

Kate said, "Thank you Professor Hugh!"

"You ladies have a good day!"

Both ladies respond, "You too!"

As they continue walking, a white male student approaches them.

"Could you girls not do that next time? It's very rude!"

Abby responds, "If we were male students like yourself, would we be considered rude for doing it?"

"Pulling the gender card.....why do you bitches do that every time a man gives his opinions?"

Kate responds, "Because of bitches like you who aren't man enough to be okay with being around smart, confident women!"

The male student just stares at them. Kate then continues.

"Now if you would excuse us, we have shit to do!"

The girls then walk away.

"Kate....are you okay?"

"Yeah.....how about you?"

"Yeah......"

They stop and start screaming and jumping. They give each other a big hug.

"Oh My God! Kate......we have an interview with Charm Vault!!!!!"

"I know! Oh God....."

"What?"

"Abby.....it's this Friday! If we're going to nail this thing....we have a lot of shit to do!"

"Oh shit.....I just realized that!"

"Yeah....but for now.....let's get a celebratory drink!"

"Sounds good to me!"

———

Kate finishes her first glass of whiskey and pours another one. She takes a big sip and starts bawling.

Kate hears the doorbell ring.

Who could that be?

Ch. 11

Betty manages to get up and answer the door....it's Evan Pale.

Betty swings her arms around him, "EVAN!!!! SHE'S GONE!!!"

" I know Mrs. Block!!!"

When Betty let's go, Evan enters the house. Mark sees Evan and gives him a hand shake. Then Evan gives him a hug.

"I'm so sorry Mr. Block."

"Thanks son."

Evan then acknowledges Andrew and Allie.

Betty then says, "I thought that your flight arrived here this afternoon."

"Well...it was supposed to. But there was a delay. Then I went by Abby's apartment and saw that her parking spot was taped off by police. That's when I saw Detectives Barns and Smith and answered a few questions."

Kate walked downstairs with a Jack Daniels bottle in one hand and an empty glass in the other. She puts both on a table in the foyer and gives Evan a big hug.

"EVAN!!!!!"

"So sorry Kate."

"So...what are you doing here Evan?"

Evan takes out a black box and gives it to Kate.

"Here....open it."

Kate opens the box. She can barely hold it.

"Evan.....you.....you...."

Betty says, "Kate what is it?"

Kate turns the black box around......it has a sizable diamond engagement ring inside.

Evan turns to Betty and Mark.

"That was going to be the surprise Mr. and Mrs. Block."

Everyone just stood there in shock.

Allie covered her mouth with her hand. She then said,

"I........I......helped him pick it out."

Betty looks at Allie.

Allie uncovers her mouth, "Excuse me y'all......"

She walks into the living room at sits on the couch. She has a flashback.

Allie is sitting in a plush chair at Winger Jewelers, an upscale jewelry store on 5th Avenue. It's one of the many stores they used to own before selling the business. She sees Evan enter. She walks over to him and gives him a big hug.

"Hi Evan! So good to see you!"

"Hi Mrs. Winger! Good to see you too! Thank you soooooo much for this!"

"Oh no problem! After all...it's my specialty."

"So glad I asked you because...this is sooo not my specialty."

Both of them laugh.

Allie continues.

"So let me tell you what Abby is into. She likes big statement pieces. She loves bling pieces with a touch of elegance. She's totally *not* into gaudy looking pieces."

She points to an oversized ring.

"Like that one for example. That ring is wayyyy too big. She would totally *not* be impressed with that one!"

Allie stops walking; she spots a perfect cushion white gold diamond ring with a beautiful diamond in the center and small diamonds around it.

"Now this.....this will be perfect. Excuse me ma'am, may I see this ring please?"

The sales woman takes the stand out with the gorgeous ring and carefully places it on a black velvet mat.

"Evan...look...at....this."

"Mrs. Winger.....it's beautiful."

"Abby is going to love this one. So what do you think?"

"I'm going to get this one for her. She will go head over heels for this one!"

"Good choice Evan!"

Allie sees Kate and Abby walking into the store.

"Evan, Evan! Abby is here!"

Allie then turns to the sales woman.

"Ma'am can you take him to the showing room in the back please. Thank you."

The sales woman nodded. "I certainly will. Um Jay, can you take this ring and prepare it for purchase? Thanks."

Evan and the woman walk into the back of the store.

"Mom?"

Allie turns around and sees Kate and Abby.

"Oh hi ladies! What are you doing here?"

"We're asking you the same question."

"Well you're father and I are founders of this company yah know."

"Mrs. Winger, is Evan here? I thought I just saw him here through the window."

"I thought I saw him too. But he was someone else."

"Okay. Kate wanna get something to eat? I'm starving! There's an Italian restaurant next door. Mrs. Winger, would like to join us?"

"Of course! Thank you! You girls go ahead I'll catch y'all in a few!"

"Okay Mom! See you soon!"

Kate and Abby leave the store.

Allie turns back to the sales woman, "Ma'am, can you bring Evan back here?"

"Of course."

"Thanks."

Evan walks up to Allie, "That was close!"

"Tell me about it! Anyway they've invited me over for lunch next door so when you walk out of here, turn left not right. Okay?"

"Okay. Mrs. Winger?"

"Yes?"

"Thanks."

Allie smiled, "You're welcome."

Allie starts bawling on the couch.

Ch. 12

Evan woke up and got out of bed. He exits his guest room in The Block's mansion. He walks down to the kitchen and starts the coffee. Evan is a software engineer at his parents' technology company in New York City. He has an apartment in the city. Unlike Abby, Evan came from old money. His parents started their company with the help of his grandparents' money. Evan turns on the news looking to see if there's a story on Abby's disappearance. There is none.

"You gotta be *fucking* kidding me?!"

"What?"

Evan turns around and sees Kate who has one hand on her head and barely putting one foot in front of the other.

"Oh.......thanks for starting the coffee. This headache Jack gave me is killing me!"

"Jack?"

"Jack as in Jack Daniels."

"Oh........well when it's ready feel free to take the first cup."

"Thanks.....what the hell are you screaming about?"

Evan points to the TV.

"Look! The anchor said not one damn thing about Abby's disappearance!"

"You gotta be fucking kidding me!"

"That's because our daughter doesn't have blonde hair and blue eyes!"

Evan and Kate turn around and see Mark dragging his feet.

Evan says, "I'm sorry Mr. Block. I'm not following."

"Boy, do you really think they care about a missing black girl?"

Both of them just look at Mark.

"With the look on your faces, you already answered that question."

Evan shakes his head, "That's real messed up."

Kate says, "She's a human being!"

"Well some don't look at our people as human beings!"

Evan pours three coffee cups, puts cream and sugar in them, and places the cups on the island.

Mark and Kate thank him.

Mark begins, "So no news coverage on our girl huh."

Evan responds, "Nothing as far as I'm concerned."

Kate freaks out, "Oh shit!!!!! What time is it?"

Evan looks at his phone, "It's 10AM."

"God damn it! I have work!"

Mark says, "Oh......"

Kate's phone rings.

"Fuck! It's Danielle!"

She picks up.

"Danielle! I'm *so* sorry! I was about to call you to tell you I need one more day off if that's okay!"

"Kate don't even worry about that. You and Abby have interned with me before so I know you would *never* leave me hanging. I was just calling you to see how you were doing."

"Um......really I feel horrible.....to be honest."

"Well....so sorry to hear that....I....didn't see any news coverage! Why is that?"

"I think both of us know the reason why."

"Yeah......so take all the time you need and I'll see you when you get back...take care of yourself Kate."

"I will. Thanks for calling. Bye."

"Bye."

Kate hangs up, "It's all good."

Mark said, "Well that's good to hear."

"Yeah....."

"But don't take too much time off. Mrs. Block and myself don't want you to put your life on hold because of this......and you know Abby certainly wouldn't want you to put your life on hold."

"I know Mr. Block......I miss her! She's my right hand! She's like a sister to me!"

Kate feels herself about to cry.

"Excuse me......"

She leaves the kitchen and takes her coffee with her.

Mark takes a sip of his coffee, "I'm gonna go upstairs to see how Betty's doing."

"Okay."

As Mr. Block leaves, Evan has a flash back.

—————

Evan approaches Abby and Kate's apartment on campus in a black button up shirt with black pants. He knocks on the door and Kate opens it.

"Hey Evan...."

"Hey Kate! Sorry to drop by here on a whim. Is....Abby here?"

"Yes! Come on in!"

Evan enters into the girls' modern style campus apartment. The living room has a black couch and two black chairs with a black rug and coffee table in the center. The kitchen has a granite countertop with wooden cabinets and a stainless steal dishwasher and fridge. It has two bedrooms and bathrooms.

As Evan sits on the couch in the living room, Kate asks him, "Do you want anything.....beer or wine or..."

"Ummmm no I'm good thanks!"

"Abby! Abby! Come out here!"

"Does it have to be right now Kate?!"

"Yeah! Just come!"

Abby exits her room and her mood suddenly changes when she sees Evan. She walks over to him and they briefly kiss on the lips.

"Evan! What.....are you doing here?"

"I was wondering if you're free tonight?"

"Where are we going?"

"It's a surprise!"

"Oh...so it's one of those nights...okay! When do we have to leave?"

"In about 45 minutes or so!"

"Okay! I'll get ready!"

"Oh and.....pack an overnight bag. Don't forget your passport."

"Okay....."

Abby walks out of her room with a mid length red dress and red sparkly heels.

"Ready sweetie!"

"Wow Abby......you look....."

Kate steps in, "Beautiful!"

Evan looks at her for a few seconds then snaps out of it.

"Well....let's get going!"

Abby gives Kate a hug, "I'll see you later!"

"Have fun you two!"

The couple walks out of the apartment complex. There is a black limo waiting out front.

Abby turns to Evan with a smile on her face, "Evan……what is going on here?"

Evan takes a long silk red cloth out of his pocket and ties it around Abby's head, covering her eyes.

"Well….you're just going to have to wait until we get to our destination."

Abby giggles.

"Okay…."

They enter the limo and drive off. It eventually stops. Evan and Abby get out of the limo.

"Evan….where are we?"

He takes off the blindfold.

Abby is at a private airport and there's a private jet right in front of her. It has *Pale Solutions* written on it, the name of Evan's parents' company.

"Evan…..is this your family's plane?!"

"Yep!"

Abby crossed her arms.

"And………how many girls have you brought up here?"

"You're the first one."

Abby uncrosses her arms. Evan walked over to her and they kiss.

When they stopped, Evan said, "C'mon, we gotta go."

"Where are we going?"

"Where you've always wanted to go."

"Turks and Caicos!"

"Yeah!"

Eva's parents have a couple of properties on the island. One of the houses belongs to Evan. Abby and Evan take their seats and have some champagne with an assortment of cheeses. They arrive at the airport and another limo takes them to Evan's beach house. The house has an incredible ocean view. It is painted in light blue with a front porch. They enter into the house and put their stuff down.

"We gotta get back in the car."

"Evan…..what's the rush?"

"I'm taking you out to dinner."

"Somewhere fancy?"

"You'll see."

They enter the limo and take off. They exit the limo and enter a restaurant on the beach.

"Evan……..you shouldn't have."

"Of course I had to. Only for the most beautiful girl in the world."

Abby smiles at Evan for a few seconds, "I just love these random trips we take on the weekends! They make me fall in love with you all over again every time."

Evan walks over to her and kisses her.

When they leave the restaurant, the couple strolls on the beach. Abby and Evan have their shoes off and let the water run over their feet as they stroll on the sand holding their shoes…..and each other's hands. They stop for a brief moment and enjoy the view of the beautiful, light blue, clear water. Abby turns to Evan.

"I love you."

"I love you too."

They both kiss again.

———

Evan takes his coffee cup and shoves it down the island. It shatters on the floor and coffee begins to flood out. He collapses on the floor and begins to cry. Kate runs to the kitchen.

"What the fuck is that?!"

She runs over to Evan and hugs him.

"Sorry.....about the coffee!"

"No worries Evan.........it's okay.......it's okay just let it out...okay."

"WHYYYYYYYY?! WHY HER?! WHY HER?! SHE'S MY FIRST LOVE!!!! IF I LOSE HER.....I WON'T KNOW WHAT ELSE TO DO!!!! WHAT WILL WE DO KATE?! WHAT WILL WE DO?!"

"I don't know Evan.......I don't know."

Ch. 13

Mark enters their bedroom and sees Betty in bed watching TV. When he walks in, he sees home videos of Abby playing in the backyard when she was little. Allie walks up to him and put her hand on his shoulder.

"How are you holding up?"

"I feel so numb right now I don't know how I'm holding up."

"Well......um.....I tidied up all the bedrooms so y'all don't have to worry about keeping up the house."

"Thanks."

Allie pauses for a few seconds and looks at Betty.

"Is she still looking at those videos?"

Mark took a deep breath.

"Yep."

"Well.....we need to snap her out of it."

Allie walks past Mark and takes the changer to turn off the TV.

Betty looks at her with wide eyes.

"Girl....what the fuck did you do that for?!"

"Because looking at those videos ain't gonna bring her back Betty."

Betty crosses her arm.

"Now....Andrew is going to be here shortly with breakfast."

"But I'm not hungry!"

"You need to eat Betty!"

"I SAID I'M NOT HUNGRY!!"

Betty starts sobbing. Allie walks over and sits on her bed.

Mark jumps in, "The news had no coverage on Abby's disappearance. That means....we have to look for her ourselves."

Allie says, "So that means you need all the food you can get to look for her. Betty.....you think that laying in this bed all day is going to bring her home?"

Mark sits on the bed too, "You know the police nor anyone in this town aren't going to care about our girl."

Betty gives him a glaring look.

"Besides Allie and her family and Evan, who has come to give their condolences?"

Betty just stares at him.

"Exactly.....which means we have to look for her ourselves."

The doorbell rings and Lala starts barking.

Allie says, "Well........Andrew is here. Better go downstairs and eat."

Mark asks, "Allie how much do we owe you for the food?"

'Mark.....c'mon you're family.....stop it. Now go downstairs and eat."

She turns to Betty.

"Both of y'all go and eat...c'mon."

Finally, Betty gets out of bed. She looks at Allie who's just standing there.

"Girl......you're rushing Mark and I to go downstairs...aren't you coming too?"

"Girl...I was waiting for you."

Betty gives Allie a hug.

"Thanks...for everything."

"You're welcome."

The three of them walk downstairs. Kate finishes sweeping the broken coffee cup in the dust pan and throws it in the trash.

Allie asks, "What is that?"

"Nothing Mom."

Allie looks at Kate for a few seconds then walks over to Andrew to help him set the table.

Allie starts taking food out of the bag and calls out, "Okay so we have.......two cheese omelets, two egg and cheese sandwiches, and two sausage egg and cheese sandwiches....all of them come with hash browns. So....dig in y'all."

As everyone started to dig in, Betty just realized something.

"Oh shit! Lala wasn't fed yet."

Allie responded, "Don't worry about that. Andrew bought a side of bacon just for her."

She takes the top off of the container and gives the bacon to Lala.

Allie puts her hand on her head, "Shit! We forgot the coffee!"

Kate cocks her head to the coffee pot, "Evan made a fresh pot of it."

"Thanks Evan."

"You're welcome Mrs. Winger."

Everyone manages to eat their breakfast when the door bell rings.

Allie gets up, "I'll get it."

She opens the door and Detectives Barns and Smith are here.

"Hi Detectives."

"Hello," said Jackie.

"Please, come in."

"Thank you," said Heidi.

The detectives enter the house. Jackie and Heidi start looking around. They enter the kitchen where everyone is eating.

Jackie says, "Hi Everyone."

Heidi says, "Hello."

Jackie says, "Betty, Mark, you have a beautiful home."

Betty responds, "Thank you."

Jackie begins, "I see that everyone is here! Detective Smith and I have a few more questions to ask."

Evan jumps in, "With all due respect, shouldn't you be looking for the person who did this to Abby instead of wasting your time with us.......the people who love and care about her deeply?"

Jackie says, "Mr. Pale, Detective Smith and I will be doing that........in order to do that, we need to find out who had a grudge against her and in order to do that......we need to find out who they are by asking the people who are closest to her...okay?"

Evan says, "I'm sorry Detective Barns....it's just that...."

Evan walks off and starts to cry.

Kate jumps in, "He was going to propose to her last night."

Jackie and Heidi cover their mouths and say in unison, "Oh my....God."

Jackie walks off to find Evan. When she finally sees him, he is slouching on the couch in the living room.

Jackie walks over, "May I sit?"

"Sure, go ahead."

Lala walks over to Jackie.

Jackie pets her, "Hey there."

"That's Lala. Her and Abby are like best buds."

"That's why they call them man's best friend."

"Again Detective Barns....I'm sorry-"

"Evan don't worry about it."

"So you wanna know who hated Abby?"

"Well I wouldn't put it in those terms...um.....is there anyone you know that didn't like her?"

"My parents certainly don't."

Jackie looked at him for a few seconds.

"I'm sure you can figure out why Detective."

"Yeah...yeah I can. I know from personal experience."

"How? If....you don't mind me asking."

"No not at all. My parents are totally cool with me marrying the woman I love. They loved her the moment I introduced her to them. My wife's parents however.......weren't too crazy about her marrying me.

Jackie took a deep breath.

"They lured her into a field only to be met by her other relatives and together they tried to *pray the gay away*. When they realized that didn't *work*, they gave her an ultimatum: either leave me and stay with the family or stay with me and the family would disown her and pretend that she doesn't exist. They hate us so much.......they don't even speak to us anymore...not even to our kids."

"Really? That's fucked up. I guess that's how my life will be.......my parents not speaking to Abby and I....and their grandkids."

Evan took a deep breath.

"A couple of months after Abby and I started dating, we've decided that it was time for us to meet the parents. She invited me over to her parents' house for dinner. Her parents loved me the moment I met them."

"They didn't care that you were white?"

"Oh no, not at all! Mr. and Mrs. Block treat me like I'm their son. Mrs. Block makes the best homemade macaroni and cheese. Whenever she invites Abby and I over, she makes separate batches for her and I. Mr. Block and I, would sit outside on the porch talking for hours over a bottle of beer."

"Abby is very lucky to have Mark and Betty as parents. They seem to care a lot about her and her friends."

"I wish my parents were the same way."

"How?"

Evan takes another deep breath.

"I'm sure you know about my family.....and their legacy."

"I sure do."

"All they're concerned about is upholding that legacy of theirs."

"Okay."

"I mean they were cool with me having friends over the house. I've had a black friend over a few times and there wasn't any issue with that. But when I came over for dinner and introduced Abby to them...let's just say that they barely ate that night. They barely said a word to her. After dinner, when I was helping my mom out with the dishes, I'll never forget what she said to me. She said, "Honey, it's one thing to be friends with them, it's another thing to date them. I mean we have a family legacy to hold up....a company to run. Do you think that our clients will continue to use our services or if our family will continue to be the crème de la crème of society if they found out that you are dating.......*a black girl*? I mean I love you dear but your father and I just can't approve of this. I hope you understand where I'm coming from."

Jackie silently winces for a few seconds and says, "What did you say?"

"I said no I don't understand because I never understood ignorance."

"Good for you."

"Can I ask you something?"

"Sure."

"How did I not end up like my parents?"

"Because you're too good of a guy to think like them."

Jackie took a deep breath and continues talking.

"What are your parents' names?"

"Jim and Jane Pale."

"Where do they live?"

"They still live in Broomville. They lived there forever. That town is maybe 1% black. I think that's why my parents moved us there."

Evan sees a pen and a pad of paper on the coffee table. He starts to write on in and gives the ripped piece of paper to Jackie.

"Here's their address."

"Thank you."

Jackie takes a deep breathe and continues talking.

"How did you and Abby meet?"

"We met at an art gallery in NYC. She was there for an assignment for her art class in college. I loved her the moment I laid eyes on her. The next thing I knew, we went to a restaurant and talked for hours over dinner. The rest is history."

"Sounds like you love her very much."

"I do. More than anything in the world."

"Evan, I have to ask you this. If you don't like your parents….why are you working at their company?"

"What other choice do I have? I can't get a job anywhere else."

"Why not?"

"Before I graduated from college, I was looking for a job at other companies. The first thing they asked me is why are you looking for a job at our company when you can just work at your family's company? After dealing with that multiple times, I just gave up and began working for my parents."

"Even if they don't approve of your relationship with Abby?"

"They're still not crazy about it and they let me know every time I see them. Like I said earlier, I really don't have much of a choice."

"A smart man like yourself always has a choice. The thing is…..do *you* believe that yourself?"

Evan just looks at her.

"Well I should get going."

As Jackie stands up, Evan stands up with her.

"Detective-"

"You can call me Jackie."

"Jackie......if there is any update, please let me know."

"If there is an update, you'll be one of the first to know."

"Thank you."

Jackie nodded her head and headed towards the foyer. She sees Heidi walking towards there too. They leave the mansion and walk to their car.

"Jackie.....are you okay?"

"Girl......after what Evan said in there about his parents, we need to pay them a visit."

"What makes you say that?"

"His parents didn't approve of his relationship with Abby.....his mom was afraid that his family wouldn't be able to keep being the creme de la creme of society if he's dating a black girl."

"His parents sound just like mine about my husband. Anyway.....I had a chance to talk to the rest of the group. The next door neighbors to the left of here called the police on the Blocks throughout the years......for having a party in their backyard. They even called during all of Abby's graduation parties. Claiming that the Blocks were making 'too much noise.' Yet the people in this neighborhood have parties all the time and they never called the police on them."

Heidi turns to the mansion and starts to speak again.

"Look Jackie! Their daughter is missing and besides the Wingers, nobody in the neighborhood has come over to express their condolences or sent flowers....or anything! It's ridiculous!"

"It's not ridiculous Heidi."

"Then what is it?"

"It's hate. They know they can't physically hurt the Block family.....but they can psychologically hurt them by making them feel like they don't belong here. That's why I get so crazy whenever people say that racism isn't as bad up here. Things aren't that much better up here.....they just have a better way of covering it up and tying it into a big ass bow."

"You're damn right about that."

"Wanna pay neighbor knuckle heads a visit?"

"Sure. Let's get it over with."

"What are their names?"

"Eric and Liz White."

Jackie and Heidi walk over to the mansion on the left of the Block's. They ring the doorbell and a Hispanic woman opens the door. She has a timid personality.

"Hi ladies. Can.....I help you?"

Heidi answers, "Hi ma'am. I'm Detective Smith and this is my partner Detective Barns. Are Mr. and Mrs. White here?"

All of the sudden a woman's voice shoots through the foyer. The Hispanic woman jumps when she hears it.

"ANGELA!! GET BACK TO WORK!!!!"

The woman walks to the foyer. She turns to Angela, who is still standing there.

"What the *hell* did I just say about-"

Heidi jumps in.

"You must be Mrs. White."

Mrs. White slowly looks at Heidi.

"Yes.....who are you?"

"I'm Detective Smith-"

"Oh you must be investigating that *black girl* that's missing around here, right?"

Heidi gives her a look and then says, "Her *name* is Abby Block, Mrs. White."

Mrs. White then turns to Jackie.

"Uh sweetie....what house do *you* belong to?"

Jackie gives Mrs. White a look and says, "Sweetie.....the house *I belong* to is the Still Vo Police Department. I'm Detective Barns."

Mrs. White jumps up, "Oh.....um....well......come in. Angela, go fetch us some tea!"

Angela puts her head down and walks over to the kitchen.

Heidi and Jackie walk into the living room that is all in silver.....like the rest of the house. Even the furniture is silver. Mrs. White sits on a couch.

"Please Detectives.....sit."

Heidi and Jackie take a seat on the couch across from Mrs. White.

Jackie begins to speak.

"So Mrs. White, we're just questioning everyone who knew the Block family. Um.......where were you the night Abby disappeared?"

"My husband and I were here having a lovely dinner."

Angela walks over with a tray that was filled with an entire tea set. She carefully places it on the coffee table.

"Thank you," said Jackie and Heidi.

Angela nodded at them and Mrs. White gave her a sneer look. When Angela notices the look on Mrs. White's face, she puts her head down and walks away.

Jackie says, "Angela is.....um.....very quiet."

"She is. I just wish she worked harder around the house."

Heidi takes a sip of tea, "The tea is very good and the tea set is beautiful."

"Oh don't credit her for that. That tea set is from my great grandmother."

Heidi said, "Well *Angela* does a wonderful job at keeping it nice and polished."

Mrs. White looks at them for a moment, "What is this *really* about detectives?"

Jackie responds, "Mrs. White, we found out that you and your husband called the police on the Block family whenever they had family events at their residence."

"Well…..they were disturbing us!"

"A graduation party……*disturbs* you?"

"Well……no…it's just that when um……"

"When the Block family……the *only* black family on this block, hosts a party…..that *disturbs* you and your husband."

"Detective Barns, we are *very* welcoming to *every* resident on this block."

"Except when they look like me."

Mrs. White looks down at her shaking hands.

Heidi jumps in, "People in this neighborhood know that Abby is missing and…….no one has…come over to the Block's house to pay their respects. No flowers or calls or anything. That includes you and your husband…that are *neighbors* to the Blocks. Do you care to tell us why that is?"

Jackie asks, "Mrs. White, are you okay? Your hands are shaking."

Mrs. White looks at them with narrowing eyes. Her hands stop shaking.

"Detectives, I think this chat should continue……..with my attorney present. So I have to ask you to leave."

Heidi and Jackie look at each other.

Mrs. White's eyes widen and she raises he voice, "Leave Detectives! Now!"

Jackie and Heidi stand up. As they reach the door, Jackie turns around.

"Mrs. White, when you're ready to talk with your attorney present, he or she can reach out to us."

Jackie takes out her card and puts it on the table by the door.

Mrs. White narrows her eyes again and says nothing. As Heidi and Jackie get to the car. They see a couple approaching the Block's residence.

Jackie says, "I…..wonder who they could be."

Heidi says, "Let's find out."

Heidi and Jackie approach the couple. They are an old Italian American couple. They are carrying bags of food.

Jackie says, "Excuse me? Sir? Ma'am?"

The couple turns around. Jackie continues.

"Hi I'm Detective Barns and this is my partner Detective Smith. Are you friends of the Blocks?"

The old woman responds, "Well.....yeah you can put it that way. My husband, Frank and I own the Pasta Lava."

Jackie and Heidi look at each other.

Frank begins to talk, "Detectives....is everything okay? My wife, Dina and I are just paying our respects. We knew the family very well. They've been our customers for years."

Jackie says, "No uh Mr..."

"Our last names are Galliano but call me Frank."

"Frank....you and your wife are fine. It's just that, Betty and Mark last saw their daughter at your restaurant."

Dina's eyes widen, "Oh my God!"

"Mrs.-"

"Please call me Dina."

"Dina we're not suggesting that you and your husband were involved at all."

"Oh we know Detective but.....my restaurant is my baby. Well.....besides my two kids. But the fact that they last saw their daughter at my restaurant. I'm just....shocked you know."

Jackie nods her head then says, "Of course. We're not going to hold you two any longer."

Dina says, "Yeah. I pretty sure it's crowded in there...people paying their respects, all of that."

Heidi says, "Yeah......Dina.....besides the Wingers. You know them right?"

"Yeah! They're good friends with the Blocks!"

Heidi nods, "Besides them and Abby's boyfriend.....you two are the only visitors really."

"No! That....that can't be!!"

Frank jumps in, "What's wrong with people?!"

Heidi says, "I ask myself the same question all the time."

Jackie jumps in, "Dina, do you have anytime to talk in the afternoon tomorrow? We're just trying to speak with people who know the family."

"Oh of course you can! Come to the restaurant at 12! We're not as busy during that time. Dinner time is usually the time we're really busy! Okay?"

"Okay with me. We'll see you tomorrow."

"See you then! Bye now!"

"Bye!"

Jackie and Heidi get into their car.

Heidi says, "Do you want to pay Evan's parents a visit?"

"Sure why not? We're already out here."

They drive off.

Ch. 14

Frank rings the doorbell. Allie answers it. She gives Frank a hug and Dina a kiss on the cheek.

"Hi Frank and Dina. Thanks for coming. I'll help you two with the food. Please come in."

The three of them walk into the kitchen.

Dina puts her hand on Allie's shoulder.

"How are you holding up hon?"

"I'm holding on as tight as I can."

"How about Betty?"

"She's as good as you would expect. I almost had to drag her out of bed this morning."

"Oh God....where is she?"

"She's in her office."

"Excuse me."

Dina leaves Allie and heads towards Betty's office. When she gets there, she sees Betty sitting on her chase lounge pouring herself another glass of Cabernet. From her demeanor, it looks like the glass of wine she's pouring is certainly not her second one.....or third.

Dina gently calls out, "Betty?"

Betty stops pouring her glass and looks up.

"Dina? Is that you?"

"Yeah hon. Can I come in?"

Betty takes a big gulp of her wine and waves her hand signaling her to come in.

"Knock yourself out."

Dina walks in and sits in a chair by Betty's desk. Betty takes another bug gulp of her wine.

"Betty.......how many glasses of wine have you had?"

Betty stops drinking and puts her glass on the small table next to her chase lounge.

"I don't know and frankly.....I don't give a fuck."

Dina just looks at her.

Betty picks up the TV changer from the table next to her and turns on the news.

"Dina look at the TV. Those fuckers at our local news station aren't even talking about Abby. It's like they don't care....oh wait.....they don't care!"

She takes another big gulp of wine and continues.

"Why don't they care about my baby?! Why?!"

Betty finishes her wine and starts bawling. The empty glass lays on her body. Then she takes that same glass and throws it across the room. It shatters when it hits the wall and the shards of glass crumble down to the floor.

Dina sits on the side of Betty's chase lounge. She turns off the TV and puts her arms out.

"Come here hon."

Betty sits up and lays her head on Dina's shoulder. She continues crying.

Meanwhile, when Frank is done putting the food out, he sees Mark sitting at his desk in his office and Frank starts walking toward him. Mark finishes drinking his glass of whiskey and pours himself another one. Frank knocks on the door. Mark looks up.

"Hey Frank. Come in, come in."

Franks walks into the office and sits in the chair on the other side of his desk.

"Mark.....I'm not going to even ask how you're holdin' up. I know that sounds.....blunt...um."

"Don't worry about it Frank. I'm glad you didn't ask me that because I won't be holding up until Abby is here. Here at home."

Frank spots papers that Mark is looking at.

"Whatcha lookin' at?"

"Trying to figure out who took Abby. I printed out emails when Betty and I had our company. I'm looking from red flags. We had some enemies throughout the years."

"Mind if I give ya a hand?"

Mark nods toward the pile of papers in front of him.

"Knock yourself out."

Mark gets up and retrieves a glass from the cupboard. He sits back down and pours a glass of whiskey for Frank and himself. He gives Frank the full glass.

"Thanks Frank."

"No problem."

The two men cling their drinks and take a sip. Then they resume their attention to the emails.

The doorbell rings again. Allie walks towards it when Kate walks down the steps.

"I got it Mom."

Kate opens the door. Her boyfriend, David, is here. Kate jumps into his arms and start kissing him.

"David! So good to see you."

She kisses him again and then plops her head on his shoulder. She begins to cry. He whispers in her ear.

"It's okay babe. It's okay."

David spots Allie and sees Andrew walk up to her. Kate jumps down from David's arms. David walks over to Kate's parents and gives them a hug.

"Mr. and Mrs. Winger. I got here as fast as I could."

Allie says, "No worries David. Thanks."

"My parents were on vacation when they got my text message. They should be here tomorrow morning to check on Mr. and Mrs. Block. How are they doing?"

Kate said, "As you expected."

Mark walks into the foyer. David and him exchange a hug.

"Mr. Block....I'm so sorry."

"Thank you."

Frank walks up to David and put his hand on David's shoulder.

"Hey David. Why don't you uh......stick around and have some food."

"Thanks Frank."

Everyone walks into the kitchen.

David Tanner has been Kate's boyfriend for three years. He grew up in an upper class African American family. His father, Bill, is a retired defense attorney. He was considered the best in New Jersey. His mother, Gayle, is a housewife. The Tanner's live in Mintville,. It's an upscale town about 20 minutes away from Still Vo. The Tanners and the Blocks have been friends for a very long time. That's how David and Kate met. The Blocks had the Wingers, and the Tanners over for dinner and Kate and David could not stop talking. David also lives in Mintville and runs his father's law practice, Tanner and Associates.

Meanwhile, Jackie and Heidi arrive at the Pale's residence. Jackie rings the doorbell and a middle-aged black woman opens the door.

"Hi ma'am. I'm Detective Barns and this is my partner Detective Smith. We're here regarding the Abby Block case. May we come inside?"

"Sure ma'am."

They enter the mansion and everything is white, even the furniture. A white woman walks into the foyer.

"Lisa, I can take it from here. Thanks."

Lisa walks off. Mrs. Pale shakes the detectives' hands and gestures them to the living room.

"Hi Detectives. I'm Jane Pale. Please have a seat."

The three women sit in the living room.

"Sorry my husband isn't here. He's on a business trip. So you're probably here to ask me some questions about Abby Block's disappearance."

Jackie answers, "Yes Mrs. Pale, we are. So where were you on the night of Abby's disappearance?"

"I was with my husband at the office. Our company is going through another acquisition. The building security guard can verify that."

Jackie slowly nods her head and continues, "Mrs. Pale…..you are aware of Evan's relationship with Abby."

"Yes and he had *nothing* to do with that girl's disappearance."

"Actually Mrs. Pale…..I wasn't insinuating that at all. Evan told me…..how you and your husband felt about Abby."

Mrs. Pale looked down at her lap and took a deep breath.

Heidi jumps in, "Would you care to elaborate?"

Mrs. Pale looks up at them and says, "Look…..I know it looks bad. Um……I don't hate Abby…I really don't. I know she makes him very, very happy. It's just……."

Jackie jumps in, "Go on."

"It's just that in our family's *network*, we would be looked down upon. I mean…….they're already whispering when we go to our annual galas. I wouldn't be concerned about Abby if she was……"

Jackie says, "White."

"I know it sounds……horrible. But we have a family legacy to keep up."

Heidi says, "Really? Because that sounds like an excuse to me as far as I'm concerned."

Mrs. Pale looks at her for a few seconds and then says, "Look I have a lot of work to do. So I have to ask you two to leave. My apologies."

Jackie and Heidi look at each other and back at her.

As the detectives stand up, Jackie puts something on the coffee table, "Okay Mrs. Pale. If you have anything that can help us, here's my card."

"Detective Barns…….please understand where I'm coming from with Abby."

"No I don't understand because I never understood ignorance."

Mrs. Pale's eyes widened, "My son-"

"Said the exact same thing when you asked for his *understanding*. Have a good night Mrs. Pale."

Ch. 15

Jackie and Heidi are sitting at their desks having coffee and plain glazed donuts. Their boss, Captain Tim Troll, walks up to them. He is a 60 something year old white man that has been working for the Still Vo Police Department for quite some time.

"Good Morning Detectives!"

"Good Morning Captain," both of them said.

"So about the uh......Abby Block case. We tried checking the video surveillance at her apartment complex. The cameras were broken at the time she disappeared."

Heidi sits back in her chair and throws her donut on a plate on her desk, "Of course they were broken."

Jackie shakes her head.

"Well ladies....it doesn't matter anyway because.....the mayor wants all hands on deck with the knocking down of garbage cans the town residents have been experiencing on their properties. So.......that means this case needs to be put on hold."

Both ladies look at each other and then face Tim.

Jackie says, "Is he serious?"

Heidi says, "He can't be."

Tim says, "Look I wish he wasn't serious but that's what he said."

Jackie stands, "Captain....Heidi and I have a couple of good leads. We just got started on this case."

Heidi stands, "Captain......give us a shot at this."

Tim takes a deep breath.

"Okay........what do you guys have?"

Heidi begins talking, "The Whites are neighbors to the Blocks. They called the police on the Block family for having regular gatherings such as Abby's graduation party."

Jackie then jumps in, "But whenever the other residents had their gatherings, they never called the police on them. Look Captain Heidi and I had a chance to speak with Liz White. The lady is a total racist. She asked me what *house I belonged to.*"

Tim said, "You gotta be kidding me!"

"As soon as Jackie and I grilled her about the calls and the fact that no one in the neighborhood has paid their respects to the Blocks, that's when she got nervous and said she wanted us to continue talking to her...with her attorney present and told us to leave. Plus Mrs. White was uh....rather mean to her maid, Angela. I mean she just yelled at her. She didn't physically assault her or anything but...it was something we've noticed."

Tim said, "Well......that doesn't surprise me. Where was she during the time of Abby's disappearance?"

Jackie said, "She said she was having a lovely dinner with her husband."

Tim formed an irritating look on his face, "Well....I have a hard time believing *that.* Jackie, research more on the White family to see what they're about."

"Will do."

"Do you ladies have anyone else?"

Jackie said, "Yeah, Evan Pale's parents, Jim and Jane. They don't approve of his relationship with Abby because they believe him dating a black girl would mess up their status in society."

Tim said, "Really?"

"Really Captain."

Heidi said, "She said that she didn't hate Abby but she's worried about the people whispering about them when they attend their *galas.*"

Tim asked, "Where was she at the time of Abby's disappearance?"

Heidi answered, "Mrs. Pale and her husband were at the office. They're doing another acquisition for their company. She said we could verify that with the building's security."

Tim put his hand on his head, "Okay Heidi verify that with the security there."

"Will do."

"Is there anything else you guys wanna tell me?"

Jackie says, "Yeah we're meeting with Frank and Dina Galliano today at the Pasta Lava. Besides the Wingers, who are very good friends with the Blocks, they were the only ones who visited the Blocks to pay their respects."

Heidi jumps in, "I had a chance to ask the Wingers, including their daughter, about their whereabouts during Abby's disappearance. The three of them were having dinner with a family friend in New York City. We were able to verify that."

"How about Abby's boyfriend?"

Jackie says, "He just came back from a business trip. We were able to verify that too."

"And her parents?"

Heidi says, "Her parents went straight home from the restaurant. Captain....they're the last people who would even do such a thing. They're good people."

"I know. It's just that I wanna leave no stone unturned. Okay so I'll leave you ladies to it."

"Thanks Captain," the both of them said.

<u>Ch. 16</u>

Jackie and Heidi arrive at Pasta Lava. When they walk in, they see staff members setting up. Dina walks out from the kitchen. The place is an authentic Italian restaurant. There are family pictures and accolades featuring the restaurant on the wall.

"Good Afternoon Detectives! Please take a seat anywhere!"

Jackie says, "Hi Dina. Thank you but we don't plan on staying that long."

"Oh Detectives I insist!"

Dina turns to one of the waitresses, "Lara, get us some water!"

Lara said, "Comin' right up Dina."

Dina turns back to the Detectives, "Please Detectives?"

Jackie and Heidi look at each other and say in unison, "Well okay."

As the three ladies sit down, Lara brings a pitcher of water and pours it in the glasses on the table.

All of them thank her.

Frank walks out of the office and heads towards the table. He sits down next to Dina.

"Hey Detectives."

"Hey Frank," the detectives said.

Jackie begins, "So we know that the Block family had dinner here the night before Abby went missing. Did the Block family look like they had any conflict between them?"

Dina said, "Oh no! Not all! They had bright smiles on their faces. They were celebrating Abby's first full time job and her....um."

Frank interjected, "Birthday."

"Yeah birthday. That's what is was."

Dina continued, "They we're happy as can be! Let's order some food!"

Heidi said, "Oh Dina that's so wonderful of you but....we're, fine we don't need anything."

Dina said, "Whenever we have people over, they always have to eat. Lara?!"

Lara walks over to the table.

Dina continues, "Bring us a dish of spaghetti with meatballs, ah.....fettuccine alfredo, ravioli, and ziti."

Lara said, "Comin' right up Dina."

Lara walks away.

Heidi continues, "So you've mentioned that the Blocks have been your customers for a while or something?"

Frank said, "33 years, for as long as they lived here in Still Vo."

Jackie asked, "Do any of the customers give them any issues?"

Dina responded, "Overall the customers are pretty nice to them...except for one couple. I forgot what their names were."

Frank responded, "Eric and Liz White. It was many years ago when they came. I had to kick them out."

Jackie and Heidi look at each other.

Heidi asks, "For what?"

Dina and Frank looked at each other.

Frank continued, "Mr. and Mrs. White were sitting next to the Blocks. Abby was maybe.........5 years old. The couple looked at the Blocks like they were disgusted by them. When one of our waitresses came over to take their order, Mr. White asked to see the owner. So when I came over, Mrs. White said out loud that she refuses to sit next to a family of monkeys. Then she had the nerve to ask me to kick *them* out. I had to ask them to leave. They were just out of their minds!"

Dina, "I never understood why people have to be so terrible to others for no reason. Oh here comes our food!"

Lara comes over with a big tray of meals and places each of them on the table.

"Thanks Lara," everyone said in unison.

Jackie has the spaghetti with meatballs, Heidi has the fettutine alfredo, Dina has the ziti, and Frank has the ravioli.

All of them take a bite.

Jackie says, "Ummmm…..this is good!"

Dina says, "Nothin' like homemade meatballs hon!"

Jackie responds, "You got that right!"

Heidi says, "Ummmmm….This is delicious!"

Dina says, "Nothin' like homemade pasta dear!"

Ch. 17

Kate wakes up at 6AM and slowly strolls into the kitchen in her high-rise apartment in Still Vo. As she brews some coffee, Kate picks up her phone.

"Hi Danielle it's Kate."

"Oh hi Kate…..how are you feeling?"

"I'm feeling good enough to come into the office today."

"Oh Kate……are you sure? You're welcome to take another day."

"Thanks for the offer Danielle but…..coming to work will certainly help me keep my mind off of Abby."

"Okay. I look forward to seeing you."

"I look forward to seeing you too. Bye."

"Bye."

Kate hangs up and takes a big sip of her coffee. When she's dressed in her work clothes, she makes some hot tea. She stands at the counter for a few seconds before she takes a bottle of vodka and a shot glass out of the cupboard. She pours the vodka in the shot glass and then pours it in her tea. She does the same thing on more time and stirs it up. She pours another shot glass of vodka in a small container, puts another tea bag in a sandwich baggie, and puts them in her work tote. Right before she leaves her apartment, she looks at herself in the mirror in the hallway. Her makeup was able to cover up her puffy face from her drinking and crying the night before. She takes her red lipstick out and puts on one swipe per lip. She looks like she hasn't drank 5 glasses of wine before she went to sleep.

When she gets into her car, her headache gets worse. It feels like someone is hitting her head with a jackhammer. She puts her hand on her head.

"Fuck! My head is *killing* me!"

She pulls out a bottle of Advil and takes four pills. She then starts the ignition and drives to work.

She parks her car in the office lot. She sees another car pull up next to her. Out comes David. Kate unlocks the car door and David sits in the passenger's seat.

I hope that this vodka tea and Advil pills will get me through the rest of the day with the bitch crew.

That's what Abby and her typically called Tammie and her group of followers at the office.

David begins speaking, "So how much time do you have before you have to go in?"

Kate looks at her phone.

"Umm...about.....45 minutes. *That should be enough time to rock your world.*"

"You mean that's enough time for *me* to rock *your* world."

"Oh shut up and fuck me will you?"

"Will anyone see us?"

"Dav.......why in the hell do you *think* we're close to the woods here? No one parks here because there's a *myth* that the company has an underground dungeon around this area."

"Oh."

Kate and David kiss and take off each other's clothes and the next thing they knew, they were both naked. David is inside Kate, making her body tense up and build up good feelings inside. Kate breathes faster and faster and she starts coming. As she starts to cum, David picks up the speed. As Kate moans get louder and louder, David starts to moan and together they start screaming. When David is done, he slides out of Kate. Still breathing hard, Kate takes his hand.

"Wait....I'm not done. I'm still-"

David interrupts her by taking his hand and sliding it up and down between her legs. He then starts rubbing her breast in the same motion as his other hand between her legs. Kate's head goes back and she starts to moan again. After she reaches her peek, she continues breathing, looking up at him and smiling......with her legs still wide open. David begins to speak....looking at Kate. He looks at what's between her legs and then looks at her face.

"Better?"

"Better."

Kate sits up, looks up at David, grabs his thing and says, "Now your turn."

Kate rubs David's already hard thing.......and gently squeezes and caresses the rest of his package. His head goes back and he starts to moan again. After he reaches his peek, they both look at each other. Kate starts crying.

"I'm such a bad person!"

David moves closer to Kate and hugs her.

"Kate no you're not."

"Yes I am!! My best friend is missing.....and God knows where the fuck she is!! Meanwhile....I'm having sex! Good sex! Great sex!! What the hell is wrong with me?! I'm having fun and she's......she's gone!!!"

"Kate....there's nothing wrong with you. After all, Abby would want you to have a great time in life......like what we just did *now*."

Kate lightly hits David on his arm, "Oh stop it you!"

They both start laughing. Then......they start putting their clothes back on. Kate looks into the rearview mirror.

"Holy shit! I look like hell!"

David kisses the crook of her neck, "I think you look beautiful......just like that flower downstairs-"

Kate interrupts him with a kiss. She stops.

"Damn it Dav! You're going to make me want to fuck you again!"

"Isn't that what you want to do?"

"Yeah....if I didn't have work today!"

They kiss some more. Kate continues talking while they're kissing.

"I would *love* you to slide *in and out* of me all day. But.......if I'm not in the office in 5 minutes.....I'm screwed. Also......don't *you* have to be at work in a few?"

David looks at his phone, "Oh shit!"

Both of them rush to get themselves together before they get out of Kate's car. Kate reapplies her lipstick.

Kate thinks: *After the time I had....maybe I won't need the tea. But....I'll take it just in case.*

She's about to step outside the car when David takes her hand.

"Babe?"

Kate looks at him.

"Take it easy today. Call me if you need anything. Okay?"

"Okay babe. Love you."

"Love you too."

They kiss one more time before leaving the car.

Kate sits at her desk and gets herself ready for the day. Tammie sees Kate and walks up to her.

"Kate.....I wasn't expecting you to come back so soon!"

Kate stands up, "Well I'm here so.......yeah."

The two stand awkwardly for a few seconds.

Tammie leans closer to Kate and starts whispering.

"Kate.......were you and David.......*doing it* in your car?"

Kate jerks her head back, "Uh.....*that* is none of *your* business!"

Tammie chuckles and says, "Well the next time you decide to....you know-"

Kate interrupts, "Have sex?"

"Have just.....a little more decorum."

Kate chuckles, "Yeah! Says the prude who's incapable of getting it in with *anyone.*"

Kate starts to laugh. Tammie's face starts turning red and she walks away.

As soon as Tammie is out of sight, Kate thinks, *Well.......I guess I need that tea after all.*

Kate picks up her tea and takes several big sips. She eyes the picture of Abby and her in Abby's backyard. Kate has a flashback during the time they were interns at the company.

———————

Abby and Kate are sitting in Abby's car having tea vodka before they head into the office. Abby starts speaking.

"So how much time do we have left until we walk in there and deal with bitch crew?"

Kate looks at her phone.

"About 15 minutes."

"Shit."

Both of them take a big sip of tea. Abby continues.

"You brought your vodka with you?"

Kate takes two small vodka filled containers out of her bag.

"Got it right here."

"Cool."

Kate stares outside for a few seconds.

"Abby....I am never going into those woods."

"Girl.....I can't count how many times Evan and I got our freak on in those woods!"

Kate turns to Abby and her eyes widen.

"No.......you......didn't!"

"The *fuck* I did!"

The two start laughing.

Kate says, "Well *fucking* cheers to *that.*"

The girls clink their mugs, take several big sips, and continue to laugh.

Kate looks at the picture and slaps it down on the desk. She then takes another big sip of her vodka tea.

Ch. 18

Betty is sleeping on her chase lounge in her office. She has an empty bottle of red wine in her arms. She wakes up to a doorbell ringing. She painfully moans and she slowly gets up from her chase lounge. She's fighting a terrible, throbbing headache as she walks to the door. It feels like someone took the empty wine bottle from her arms and slammed it on her head. The doorbell rings again.

"I'm coming damn it! Give me one fucking second!"

With a hand on her head, she walks past Mark's office and sees him still looking through the pile of emails. She sticks her head in.

"Uh Earth to Mark?! Don't you hear the fucking doorbell ring?!"

Mark looks up at her.

"Betty.......I haven't had *any* sleep these past couple of days. Do you *really* think I'm in the mood to answer the-"

Betty interrupts and holds up her hands, "Never *fucking* mind. I'll get it!"

Betty finally gets to the door and opens it. Bill and Gayle Tanner are there. Gayle starts to speak.

"Girl........"

Betty falls into Gayle's arms and starts bawling. Bill puts a hand on Betty's shoulder and then walks away to find Mark. Bill sees him sitting at his desk.

"Hey Mark......"

Mark looks up.

"Hey Bill."

"Whatcha got there man?"

"I'm looking at emails I've had over the years when Betty and I had the firm. Frank helped me out the other day. We found several people who we had....let's say.....a little *trouble* with."

Mark picks up a small pile of papers in front of him and continues.

"Greg Troll: He was a client of ours; about in his mid thirties or so. He founded a luxury clothing line. He was stalking Betty. He would show up unexpectedly at our office with flowers to give to her. I told him that if he didn't stop showing up at our office, we would have no choice but to drop him as a client. Then it got worse. I was upstairs when he showed up at our house. I overheard him profess his love for Betty, and asked if she would leave me and run off to marry him. Betty screamed at him to get out of here and told him he was crazy. As he was talking to Betty, I got my 9 millimeter out of the safe, ran downstairs, and pointed it at him. I told him that if he didn't leave right this minute, I would blow his fucking brains out. Right after that, Greg ran off."

"You didn't call the police?"

"Man, you know how they feel about us here."

Bill hesitates for a second and then says, "Oh right."

Mark continues, "Frank and I found two others that were our employees. One employee was Charlie Snooper. He was in his mid twenties. Charlie sent emails to some of our female employees, commenting on their private parts and telling them how beautiful they must be beneath their work clothes. Human Resources conducted an investigation and we ended up terminating Charlie."

"Damn man....that's creepy."

"You won't think so after I tell you about Mary Naples. She was in her mid sixties or so. She was a receptionist for our office. At first she was a wonderful employee. She showed up early for work, never missed a day, and performed really well at her job. Then she came into my office one day and professed her love for me. Which was strange because she never gave me such indication before. I told her that her comments were very inappropriate and I certainly don't and have never felt that way about her. She left my office. The next day, she didn't show up at her designated time for work. We called her and she picked up the phone saying that she's running late and she would be there as soon as she could. When she showed up, she had a trench coat on. We didn't think anything of it until she walked into my office and took the trench coat off. She was completely naked from head to toe.....with heels on.....but still."

There was a moment of silence in the room, then Bill finally spoke.

"Damn man.......and I thought I had some crazy employees in the past. "

"Right."

"So......what do you think you're going to do with all of this?"

"I'm thinking about seeing these fuckers myself. Find out if they had anything to do with Abby's disappearance."

"Mark......are you sure you wanna do that?"

"Bill, I have two options. I can either sit here on my ass just waiting for my daughter to come home, or I can be proactive and look for her myself. Which one would you choose if David went missing?"

Bill didn't say anything.

"Exactly."

The doorbell rings.

Mark gets up from his chair and says, "I got it!"

He opens the door and sees a bunch of young black men and women.

Mark says, "Can I help you?"

A young woman starts to speak, "Hi Professor Block. My name is Fran Teller and I am the President of the Black Student Union at Tumble Top University. I was in you're *The Experience of Minorities in Corporate* class last semester."

"Oh yes! Fran! I do remember! Sorry my mind has been a mess lately. I would say it is so good to see you but due to the circumstances......"

"Professor Block.....that's why we're here. We heard about Abby and we wanna help look for her. Since no one is doing search parties around here we thought we might help out."

"Oh thank you! That's really thoughtful of you. Um.....how did you hear about Abby?"

"We saw a news segment about her yesterday. It was about maybe.......10 seconds."

Mark chuckled, "I'm shocked that the news even did a segment on her."

There's a moment of silence. Then, Mark speaks again, "Oh uh......please come in!"

Fran and the rest of the group enter the mansion. Once they're inside, they see Betty and Gail at the kitchen counter drinking coffee. Betty starts talking.

"Mark....who are these people?"

"Sweetie, it's the Black Student Union at the college. They're here to help look for Abby."

Betty gets up from her chair, walks over to Fran and gives her a big hug.

"Thank you."

"Of course Professor Block."

Betty let's go of her.

Fran says, "Okay everyone. Let's get started. Joe, do you have the flyers?"

Joe takes a bunch of papers out of his bag, "Got them right here Fran."

"Good."

Betty says, "I'm going upstairs to get ready. I'll be ready shortly."

Fran says, "Professor Block....take your time.....no rush."

Betty nods and starts heading towards the staircase. Gail follows her.

Betty is dressed with hot curlers in her hair. She sits at her vanity and starts to put on her makeup. Gail sits on her bed. Betty begins talking.

"When Mark and I were in our NYC apartment back in the day, we were dying to move into a gorgeous house like this. It was about 9 in the morning on a Saturday. We were having our coffee and reading the newspaper. All of the sudden, our real estate agent called. She said, 'You guys have to come and see this beautiful house! Look I know it's early on a Saturday morning but.......you two have to come now and see this!' Mark wrote down the address and we rushed into the parking garage in our pajamas and rushed out to New Jersey. When we got here.....oh Gail......we couldn't believe what we were looking at! This was the biggest house I have ever seen in my entire life! The fact that I grew up in a small apartment in a working class town; only to be able to afford all of this was just.........unbelievable! We walked throughout this place and Mark and I decided to buy it. Several days later...we got the house! Then before we knew it, we were expecting Abby."

Betty stops what she's doing, takes a deep breath, and continues.

"Seeing Abby run around the house and in the backyard was the best thing that ever happened to me! There's nothing like seeing your child happy and having all the opportunities you didn't have growing up, knowing that the world is her oyster. "

Betty finished her makeup and took out her rollers. When her and Gail went back downstairs, Detectives Barns and Smith are there.

Betty says, "Jackie....Heidi....what are you doing here?"

Jackie begins to speak, "Well we're here because we've heard of a search party going on here. So do you mind if.....Heidi and I join?"

"Oh of course you can!"

Jackie continued, "Is your husband here?"

"Yes. He's in his office."

"Thanks."

Jackie and Heidi see Mark in his office and enter.

Jackie says, "Hi Mark! Uh.....can Heidi and I have a word?"

"Sure. Please take a seat."

All three sat at his desk.

"So uh......what can I do for you detectives?"

Jackie says, "Mark......it has come to our attention that you have been looking for suspects in Abby's disappearance."

Heidi jumps in, "More like your former employees."

"Damn Frank! He was the only person who helped me go through the emails from my company!"

Heidi continues, "Technically, we're not supposed to even share this with you but......we were able to speak to Greg, Charlie and Mary. All three of them had alibis that checked out the night Abby went missing. So they are not suspects at this time."

"Okay."

Jackie says, "Mark.....we really want to find your daughter. But, investigating this case behind our backs....is not helping us at all."

"Well Jackie with all due respect.....the police department here hasn't been very fair to us over the years."

Jackie says, "Well.........not all of us are like that Mark."

Heidi says, "We're not. We have kids ourselves."

Heidi takes out a family picture with herself, her daughter and her husband. Jackie takes out her family photo with herself, her wife, and her son and daughter. Mark takes both pictures and sits back into his chair.

He speaks to Heidi, "How do your parents feel about you marrying a brother?"

Heidi takes a deep breath, "His parents loved me the second I met them. My parents.....well that's a different story."

Mark shakes his head and then directs his attention to Jackie, "How about you?"

Jackie looks at Heidi and says, "My parents loved her to moment they met her. Her parents.....we don't even speak to them anymore."

"What a damn shame. Did you know that Abby's boyfriend's parents don't like her for the same reason why your parents don't like your husband Heidi?"

Heidi responds, "Yes...we're aware of that."

"Are they suspects?"

"Their alibi checked out too. So no they're not."

Mark takes a deep breath, "I just want to find her. She's my life! I want her here! She belongs here....with her family!"

Jackie says, "Mark, we will do *anything* ad *everything* in our power to find Abby. But....you have to give us a chance....okay?"

Mark looks down and nods, "Okay."

Heidi asks, "So where is this search party going to take place?"

Mark looks up at the detectives.

Heidi says, "Why else do you think we're here?"

Mark said, "Well.....okay then! Let's join the rest shall we."

The three of them stand up. Mark asks another question.

"Wait.....the uh....pool of blood......is that......?"

Jackie says, "DNA came back. It is Abby's."

Mark says, "Oh um…….wow. I was…..hoping it was not Abby's…….you got it pretty fast. I though it would take some time."

Heidi says, "Someone in the lab owed me a favor."

Mark says, "Thank you."

They left the office and went into the living room. Besides, everyone else, they see Frank and Dina setting up the counter full of delicious food. Andrew and Allie Winger are mingling amongst Betty and Gail. Mark begins to speak.

"Hello Everyone! Uh….thanks for coming. We have…..detectives Barns and Smith here to help us out."

Fran Teller speaks, "Guys…I think it will be better if Detectives Barns and Smith run the search party since they know the town well. What do you guys think?"

Everyone agreed in unison.

"Okay then! Detectives take it away!"

Heidi takes a flyer with Abby's graduation picture on it. It shows Abby wearing a black shirt with a pearl necklace and earrings on. Her hair has big curls in it like it always does when she puts roller in it. Heidi holds the flyer up and starts to speak.

"Okay everyone! Let's start by going up door to door and showing these flyers to neighbors. Find out if they've seen or heard anything that could help us."

Fran asks, "Wait…..detectives where are the rest of your people?"

Heidi responds, "Our squad members care about this as much as how long it takes for trees to grow their full size."

Jackie jumps in, "And I think all of you know why that is."

The crowd looks at each other. Heidi continues.

"Then, we can look around the woods and walk through them. Then we can come back and have this lovely dinner Frank and Dina have for us. Sound good?"

Everyone agrees in unison.

Heidi says, "Cool. Let's get crackin'."

Everyone, except for Frank and Dina, start to leave. Kate enters the house and walks up to her mom.

Allie asks, "How did you get here?"

"Danielle let me off early. I found out about this through the campus notifications I still get from the Black Student Union."

Allie looks at her.

"Look Abby gave me their email so I can sign up for their events they have. Abby and I went to them."

Allie gives Kate a hug.

"I love you so much sweetie."

"Love you too Mom."

Jackie walks up to Kate.

"Hey Kate! Glad you could make it! Where.....are the rest of your coworkers? Are they running late?"

"They're not running here at all."

"Um....that's strange."

"Not if you're a black girl in corporate America......or a white girl in corporate America dating a black guy. Anyway......I found this in Abby's desk drawer."

Kate takes a blue notebook out of her bag and gives it to Jackie.

Jackie says, "It's Abby's journal."

"I thought you might wanna read it."

"Thanks Kate."

Evan and Dave arrive. Dave kisses Kate on the lips and gives Allie a hug. Evan walks over to Betty and gives her a hug.

Fran says, "Okay everyone! Let's go!"

The crowd leaves Betty and Mark's mansion and ventures out in the neighborhood. They start knocking on doors. Here's how it went:

"Hey. We're looking for Abby Block who is missing. Have you seen her anywhere?"

They show the flyer to them.

"No we haven't seen her anywhere sorry."

They shut the door in their faces.

Fran walks up to Eric and Liz White's mansion. She rings the doorbell. No answer. She rings the doorbell again. She hears Liz's voice through the door.

"I'm coming! I'm coming give me one damn minute!"

Fran hears a woman gurgling.

Liz says, "Oh shut up you little *bitch*!"

Fran then hears a thump. Fran turns around and sees Jackie and Heidi and runs up to them and points at the house.

"Hey Detectives!! I heard something going on in here. I don't think it's good!"

Jackie and Heidi rush to the entrance. They hear yelling. They take out their guns.

Heidi turns to Fran, "Fran, go across the street with the others okay?"

"Okay."

Fran leaves the doorstep. Jackie talks into her speaker.

"This is Detective Barns with the Still Vo Police Department. I need backup at 33 River Court Still Vo, New Jersey. Now!"

Heidi takes a step back and kicks down the door.

They barge into the mansion and see Liz beating Angela with a steel baseball bat.

Jackie and Heidi point their guns at her.

Jackie yells, "LIZ!"

Liz stops and looks up at the detectives. Her face, hands, arms, hair, and clothes are covered in blood.

Jackie continues, "PUT THE BASEBALL BAT DOWN NOW!"

Liz drops the baseball bat on the floor. Jackie continues.

"KEEP YOUR HANDS ABOVE YOUR HEAD AND GET DOWN ON YOUR KNEES!"

Liz falls down to her knees with her hands up. Heidi keeps pointing her gun at Liz as Jackie puts her gun back on her hip and cuffs Liz.

Heidi has a look of horror on her face as she looks at Angela. Her head looks like a pruned fruit covered in blood. Her hair is sopping wet from her blood. You can't even recognize her face.

Heidi walks over to feel for a pulse. She looks at Jackie and shakes her head.

Liz slowly forms a sneaky smirk on her face and says, "She's an *illegal alien*! What do you care?"

Heidi swats Liz on the head. Captain Tim Troll walks into the room. He forms a look of horror on his face. Other officers roll in and they do the same thing.

Liz says, "Uh.....did you see what she did to me?!"

Sarcastically, Tim says, "I didn't see anything."

Liz's eyes widen. Eric, her husband, appears with his back towards the officers dragging a screaming small child on the floor.

He says, "Liz.....this kid bit me again. What do you wanna do with this illegal little chicken shit?!"

Jackie, Heidi, Tim, and the other officers look at each other for a few seconds.

Tim finally says, "I should whack *you* instead you chicken shit!"

Eric turns around and his eyes widen. He drops the kid and approaches Tim. All of the officers point their guns at him.

Heidi says, "Don't you fucking DARE make another move! Get on your knees."

Eric just stands there.

Heidi continues, "GET ON YOUR KNEES NOW!!"

Eric falls to his knees and one of the officers cuffs him.

Tim says, "Get these two mother fuckers outta here now! Make sure you state their rights! I want no stone unturned!"

Several officers took Eric and Liz out of the house.

The child Eric was dragging on the floor finally got up. He looked like he has eaten very little in weeks. He looks at Angela's body horrified. He starts to shake. Jackie begins speaking to him in a comforting tone, reaching out with her arms, she says, "Hey sweetie. It's okay. It's okay. You're safe now. Come here. It's okay sweetie."

The child slowly walks towards Jackie.

Jackie asked, "What is your name?"

"Hector."

"How old are you Hector?"

"Five."

"Where is home for you sweetie?"

"Mexico. I want to see Mommy!"

Hector gives Jackie a hug and starts to cry.

Jackie says, "It's okay. It's okay."

Jackie carries Hector in her arms. She says, "I'm getting him away from this."

Tim says, "There's an ambulance truck right outside."

"Thanks."

As Jackie leaves the house with Hector, Heidi says, "Tim, I'm going to look around the house for clues as to what the *hell* is going on here......if that's okay."

"I'm coming with you."

"Tim.....my gut is telling me that we should check the basement."

"Okay."

Tim turns to everyone else, "Listen up people! Heidi and I are going to check the basement. You all should split up and check *every* single room in this house. Got it? Oh....and can someone get CSU down here?"

Everyone agrees in unison.

"Good. Let's get to it!"

Officers split up and check out different rooms.

Heidi and Tim go down the basement. At first, it looks like a normal living room with a plush couch set and a flat screen TV. Then they see a silver heavy door in the wall with a metal lock on it.

Heidi said, "I wonder what's in there."

"Let's find out."

Tim walks towards the exit and yells, "Hey! We need some pliers down here to open a lock!"

As soon as two officers break the lock, Heidi, Tim, and the two officers went inside. It was dark and damp behind that silver heavy door. As they walk down the hallway, they spot two heavy metal doors in front of them.

Heidi opens the door on the left and behind the door was a big room with a bunch of people chained up to metal bars. There had to be at least 50 of them. They all started freaking out. Heidi calms them down.

"Hey. It's okay. It's okay. We're the police. We're here to help."

Tim briefly walks out of the room and yells, "Hey! We need medical assistance down here now!"

Shortly, medical help was getting the people out of their shackles and leading them upstairs. Some of the people were dead. The medics predicted it was starvation and dehydration. As everyone was going into the ambulance trucks a frail woman in her thirties approaches Heidi.

"Hi umm......sorry dear what's your name?"

"Heidi. We should get you into an ambulance truck okay?"

"No, no. Not until you hear my story first. You have to know what happened!"

"But you don't look too well."

"Please Heidi! Please!"

Heidi took a deep breath.

"Okay. Let's sit inside the house…if that's okay."

"Sure."

Both ladies went into the living room and sat on the couch.

Heidi said, "So what's your name?"

"Anna Torres."

"So Anna…..what happened?"

"I was crossing the border with my son. Our feet were hurting so much from walking. We were so very tired. We were escaping all the violence going on in my neighborhood. As soon as I crossed over, Hector and I just laid there on the soil saying to ourselves, *We're free.* Then we saw this very nice couple, Eric and Liz. Well……at least I thought they were nice. They drove up in a big black car. Liz came out of the car. She smiled and gave each of us a bottle of water. She said, "Do you and your son need a safe place to stay until you get on your feet?"
I mean of course I said yes. So Hector and I got in the car. When we pulled up to the house, it was like a dream. Oh sooooo big and fancy. We were going to have a wonderful life here in America! We got inside and they gave us a nice meal. Then they showed us to our rooms. Hector and I each had our own rooms. I went to sleep in my cozy bed. I woke up……."

Anna began to cry. Heidi put her hand on her back.

"I woke up and……my wrists were tied behind my back. I was screaming help to find out if anyone could help me. I saw Liz and Eric standing over me………..Liz had a steel baseball bat. Eric held me down and Liz started beating me with a hot metal bat. It hurt so much! Liz simply said, *That's what you Mexican trash get for coming into this country illegally.* They did that to all of us everyday. Sometimes the bat was steaming hot. Other times it was ice cold. We were always down there in the basement. They gave us one very small meal a day and one cup of water a day……sometimes every other day. Angela was the only one that was allowed to be upstairs. When Eric was tired of Liz, he used Angela for……his needs. Oh the things he would do to her……rape her repeatedly…… She crossed the border by herself. She didn't have anyone with her. Her boyfriend back in Mexico was very abusive to her. He would hit her all the time, even broke several of her teeth. She did it to escape him and start a new life. But she was brought here the same way I was. Oh Liz *hated* her the most. When Eric was away, Liz stripped Angela naked and whipped her

93

repeatedly. I know all of this because ever time Liz put her in the dungeon with the rest of us, she would tell me what happened to her. We became friends. When and if we got out, I was going to have her join me and my son.....make her a part of my family."

Anna started crying again.

"She was a sweet girl! Why did that *bitch* kill her?! Why?!"

Heidi put her hand on her shoulder again.

"I just wanna see my son!!! Where is he?! I wanna see my Hector!"

Anna plopped her head on Heidi's shoulder and started bawling. Heidi put her arms around her.

"It's okay Anna. It's okay. You're going to be okay."

Heidi waved at an officer to come to her. She whispered in his hear.

"If Jackie is still outside, can you tell her to come here with Hector please? Thanks."

A few minutes later Jackie enters the living room carrying Hector in her arms. He turns his head.

"Mommy!"

Anna raised her head from Heidi's shoulder.

"My......my son! My son is alive?! Hector! Hector my baby!"

She looks up at Heidi and gives her a kiss on the cheek.

"Thank you sweetie! Thank you!"

Anna gets up, walks up to Jackie, and gives her a kiss on the cheek too.

"Thank you sweetie! Thank you!"

Anna takes Hector into her arms.

"Mommy! Mommy! Mommy!"

"Oh Hector! It's okay! You're safe now! You're safe! It's okay baby! It's okay! I love you so much! I missed you so much!"

They both started to cry.

An officer walks over to Jackie. She says, "I'm going to take these two to the hospital."

Anna overhears and says, "Oh I'm not leaving my son's side ever! He's staying right here with me!"

The officer says, "Ma'am I'll make sure that you're with your son the entire time at the hospital okay?"

"You promise? Because I can't have my son taken away from me again. Please!"

"Ma'am, I have two kids at home with me. I *promise* you that you will be with your son at the hospital the whole time. Okay?"

Anna nodded, "Okay. Hector....we're going to the hospital now okay?"

"Okay Mommy. You're staying with me right?"

"Yes sweetie."

Anna gives Hector a kiss on his head.

They begin to walk out and the officer puts an arm around Anna. As they get to the door, Anna sees Angela's body. She stops for a second and starts crying.

"Angela......I'm sorry I wasn't able to save you! You may be with God now......watching over Hector and I. I love you. I'm sorry!"

The officer gently says, "Ma'am.....c'mon it's okay. We have to go now, okay? C'mon."

The three of them leave the house.

Heidi buries her head in her lap and starts to cry. Jackie sits right next to her and starts crying too. Tim walks over.

"Are you two alright?"

Heidi looks up at him, "Angela........how could we not have seen it?"

Jackie looks up, "I mean......she didn't have any bruises or showed any signs of physical abuse when we were here."

"We knew that Liz was not very nice to her but what she did to her.......repeatedly whipped her. Eric.........raping her repeatedly. Liz........beating all of them daily with a hot or ice cold baseball bat *everyday.* They starved the adults and.......

"They starved the children......who......who in the *hell* in their right mind would do that to a child?"

Heidi looks at Jackie, "What?"

Tim covered his mouth, "Oh my god."

"Anna told me everything...about what Angela went through......about what she herself and the others went through......"

Jackie said, "Hector told me that they kept all the children in a separate room. Half of them are dead due to starvation. Eric and Liz fed them meals and gave them water twice a week. They also beat them everyday too with either a hot or cold baseball bat. Hector and the kids who survived, they ate their meals and drank their water a little at a time instead of taking it in all at once. He tried to tell the other kids to do the same but they didn't listen to him........"

Tim sits on the coffee table across from them and says, "Liz made sure that you two didn't see the signs of abuse on Angela. It's not your fault. Look.........you got more than enough evidence to nail these two bastards. Focus on that. Do it for Angela. Do it for Anna and Hector. Okay?"

They both nodded.

An officer came up to the three of them, He says, "You guys have gotta check this out."

As the three of them follow the officer, Tim, Heidi and Jackie look at the filled large......and small body bags that are being rolled out on stretchers. They walk upstairs into a room. It was a dark room painted in red. The room is full of news articles of white Americans who were murder victims of illegal immigrants. There is a big sign on one end of the room that read, *Close Our Borders!* On another end of the room there is another sign that read, *Build The Wall!* On another end of the room, they saw a sign that read *White Is Always Right!* On the last end of the room, the sign read *Eugenics Rules!* There is a bulletin board that has a big map of the United States on it. A route is drawn on it. The starting point is Still Vo and it ends at a town in Texas right where the Mexican border is. At the top of the map, it reads, Operation Immigrant Termination! Next to the map, there is a logo. It is a white rectangle with the letters, WMLS in black.

Tim, Jackie, and Heidi stand in the middle of the room with their jaws dropped.

Tim says something first.

"What the fuck?"

Then Heidi.

"What is all of this shit?"

Lastly, Jackie points at the rectangle with the initials on it.

"What do those letters stand for?"

She walks over to it for a closer look. She turns around and looks at Tim and Heidi, who look shocked from her behavior.

Jackie says, "Look....a black lesbian like me faces this shit everyday. So....excuse me if I don't flinch at this shit."

She turns back around to look at the map.

"Wow............so these bastards drove *all* the way from the Garden State to the Mexican border........to kidnap undocumented immigrants, bring them here......and basically torture them to death."

The officer who led them up there says, "We were able to get a count of the number of immigrants they kidnapped, fifty adults and fifty children. Twenty-five adults and twenty-five children were dead when we found everyone in the dungeon."

Jackie says, "Officer......did you find Abby anywhere?"

"No Detective. We looked for her everywhere. Couldn't find her."

He shakes his head and continues.

"Terrible.....just terrible. I know our immigration system is broken but.......this shit..........this is fucked up. No one deserves to be treated like this.......even if they are undocumented."

Ch. 19

Tim, Jackie, and Heidi are together in Tim's office.

"Look ladies.......I think we should wait and question Eric and Liz White tomorrow. Both of you......well......all of us could use some rest."

Jackie says, "Captain.....I'm tired out of my mind but.......I'm ready to take down those two bastards right now. I don't know about Heidi but....."

Heidi jumps in, "Look.....I'm ready too. Let's get this over with Captain!"

"Are you both sure?"

They say yes.

Heidi asks, "Captain, how do you want us to do this?"

"Your call ladies."

The both of them look at each other, "Really?"

"Yeah. So....what do you wanna do?"

Jackie says, "I think Heidi should question Eric, you should question Liz, and I should stay outside observing both interviews."

"Why am I questioning Liz?"

"Liz will respond better to men. She *clearly* despises women. I figure she would be more likely to open up to you than to Heidi and I."

"And why are you observing? I'm surprised you don't have me doing that."

"Captain.......we're dealing with bigots here. So I figure I play the wild card....see which interview I'll drop in on. You know.....shock them a little."

"Umm.......good call! I like it!"

Heidi says, "Me too!"

Ch. 20

Jackie observes Heidi's interview with Eric. Heidi enters the room and looks at Eric who is sitting at the table. Heidi sits down across from him and begins.

"Eric, Eric, Eric. Good news! Anna told us *everything*. How you and your wife beat the hell out of the undocumented immigrants *you both* kidnapped from the Mexican border. How you *repeatedly raped* Angela. How you separated Anna and the other immigrants from their *children*. So Eric……..what the *fuck* is going on here?"

Eric sits back and slowly forms a sneer grin on his face.

"Look Detective……I don't know why this is a big deal. They're *illegal aliens* for God sake! My wife and I are doing this great country of ours a favor! Our immigration system is broken. People are talking about how……opening our borders to these people matches our American values. That…..this country was built by immigrants."

Heidi sits back.

"Well…….this country *was* built by immigrants. Give me your tired….your poor……..isn't that how your ancestors got here?"

"My ancestors weren't dirty drug lords and rapists-"

"Really…….I thought you were a rapist."

Eric shakes his head.

"Detective…….shouldn't you be getting this?"

"Getting *what*?"

He smiles again. This time…….a more *uplifting* one.

"I mean…….you are an all American girl with your blond hair and good old European roots! You and I have the *good* genes. You see……..our people running this great country of ours are the reason why it is soooo great! I mean if we have niggers or any other people of that *dirty* skin color of theirs that come from filth and have stupidity genes running through their veins and their ancestors who come from uncivilized countries outside of good old Europe…….this country would be as terrible as they are! My wife and I had a good thing running in our house. *One hundred* illegal aliens that can't infiltrate our country and ruin it…..starved and beat them until their heart beats gave up……it's *brilliant!* You know what……..instead of a wall at the border……we should build a center that *looks* like an immigration center……..but instead of processing them and having them fill out paperwork…..we should just cut their heart beats right there and *secretly* bury them under the center. That way…….no dirty skin coloreds can ruin what this great country is! Oh and by the way……that Angela girl…….my wife and I haven't had sex in awhile. Drives me crazy! So Angela and I had a good time! Well….she was screaming and saying no…..you know…..colored people like that don't have *any* feelings. They're animals! Well…..at least I know what those animals are good for! Right?! Am I right?!"

Heidi keeps the shocked, terrified look on her face ever since Eric started his rant.

She shakes her head, "You sick son of a bitch."

Keeping that look on her face, Heidi gets up to leave the interrogation room.

"Wait……I can go now right?"

Heidi turns around and pushes the table away from the two of them, banging against the wall to the left of her. Heidi then approaches Eric who is still sitting and has a look on his face like he just shit himself. She puts her hands on her knees to meet his eye level.

"The only place you're *going* is prison. Luckily for you New Jersey no longer has the death penalty. But unluckily for you you'll be spending the rest of your *life* in prison. Speaking of prison, you'll sure get a beating since prison is mostly populated by black men and once they hear what kind of person you are……*they will want to eat you alive!* Frankly……I don't blame them."

"Fuck you *nigger lover!*"

Heidi slaps Eric hard. Jackie walks in.

"Heidi……go take a walk."

Heidi turns her head to Jackie.

"I'm not done!"

"Heidi!"

Heidi takes a deep breath and turns to look at Eric, who looks like he got caught with his pants down. She walks away from him. Jackie puts an arm on her shoulder. Heidi brushes it off.

"I need a minute."

Heidi then walks away.

Jackie sees an officer and says, "Officer, take Eric White and put him in a holding cell."

"Sure Detective."

"Thanks."

The officer enters the room and grabs Eric by the arm. The both of them walk out. Jackie then walks over to the interrogation room where Tim and Liz are. Liz is talking and looks at her hands on the table.

"I really don't know what you're talking about."

"Really..........? *One hundred* immigrants were locked up in you and your husband's mansion.......and you have the *nerve* to deny it?! Children died Liz.......*children*! How can you *explain* your way out of that?!"

"Like I said.......I don't know what you're talking about."

Jackie enters the room and stands in the corner.

She says, "Liz......your husband is something."

"I don't know-"

"Shut up! Your husband told my partner Heidi *everything.* He basically confessed to what you two were doing."

Liz finally looks up shocked.

"What?! That......stupid bastard!"

"Yeah. yeah, yeah. Look.....when we were in that red room of yours, we noticed a sticker on your bulletin board with the letters, WMLS. Care to tell us what those initials stand for?"

Liz stands up and charges at Jackie. Jackie pushes her and Liz lands on the floor. Jackie then walks over to her, squats to meet her at eye level, and says:

"You *really* don't like me do you? Guess what? I don't like your ass either."

"You know what? My husband and I didn't pull ourselves up by the bootstraps to have a nigger family as neighbors and.........*having to deal with it!*"

"Liz……did you kidnap Abby Block?"

"Of course I didn't! Why the hell do you think my husband and I took those illegal aliens? Because unlike that nigger *Abby*……..no one is going to care about them! So…….we decided to go on the illegal immigration route instead. You see Abby has US citizen documentation, family, friends, people who give a damn about her and she can be easily found. Illegals…….well…..that's another story. They come here leaving everything behind. They have no documentation. They're the perfect victims for the perfect plan!"

She then forms a smirk on her face.

Jackie has a disgusted look on her face.

"Last time Liz. What do the letters WMLS stand for?"

"You can kiss my ass……….*Detective Nigger!*"

Jackie stands up and chuckles.

"At least I'm a free nigger. Meanwhile……you'll be a locked up *skinhead cracker.*"

Liz gets up and charges at Jackie. Jackie grabs Liz and throws her down on the table.

"Girl……I thought you knew better than to charge at me like that when I pushed your ass the first time you did it."

Tim walks over with handcuffs in his hands.

"Jackie……let me take it from here okay?"

She looks at Tim and lets go of Liz. While Tim cuffs Liz, Jackie leaves the room.

Ch. 21

Jackie enters her house exhausted. She and her family live in a more affordable neighborhood in Still Vo. She enters the kitchen and sees her wife, Jennifer, and two kids, Ashley and Eddie wrapping up dinner. The kids see Jackie and run up to her.

"Mommy!"

"Hey you two!"

Jackie gives them a hug.

Jennifer, stands up and says, " Hey you two! Time for bed. Go brush your teeth."

The kids head upstairs. Jennifer walks up to Jackie and kisses her on the lips.

"Hey sweetie. How was your day?"

Jackie walked to the living room and sat on the couch. Jennifer sat next to her.

"Terrible. This couple kidnapped undocumented immigrants from the southern border and tortured and starved them to death. I mean some of them survived but....some didn't."

"Holy shit! Are you serious?"

"Yeah.....and some of them were children."

"Did the children survive?"

"Some did some didn't."

"Jesus Christ!"

Jennifer gets up from the couch and returns with a bottle of Jack Daniels and two glasses. She pours the whiskey in each glass and gives one to Jackie.

"Thanks."

Then Jackie drank several big gulps and finally put the glass on the table...finished. She pours another glass of whiskey and takes a sip of it. Jennifer only took two sips.

"I'm getting ready for bed Jen. Good night. Love you."

"Okay. Love you too."

They give each other a kiss and Jackie heads upstairs with her drink.

Ch. 22

Heidi enters her house. She and her family live in the same neighborhood as Jackie and her family. Her husband is by the door with a glass of whiskey for her. She takes the drink and gives her husband, Jordan, a kiss on the lips.

"Thanks honey."

Heidi then drinks the whole thing in a few gulps. She puts the glass on the kitchen counter when she sees her daughter, Sarah, finishing dinner. Sarah runs up to her.

"Mommy!"

Heidi carries Sarah in her arms.

"Hey sweetie!"

Jordan says, "Okay Sarah. Brush your teeth and get ready for bed."

"Okay Daddy."

Heidi puts Sarah down and she runs upstairs.

Heidi finds the Jack Daniels bottle in the cabinet and pours another glass of whiskey. She takes a sip and sits down on the couch in the living room. Jordan pours himself a glass of whiskey, takes a sip, and sits next to Heidi.

He says, "So......how bad was today? You didn't sound so good when you called me."

"Awful. This couple kidnapped undocumented immigrants from the southern border and tortured them to death. Some of them survived but....some didn't."

"What?!"

'Some of them were children. Some of the kids lived.....some didn't."

Heidi and Jordan take another sip of their drinks.

Heidi continues, "Just when I think this world couldn't get any crazier.......this shit pops up."

Jordan says, "I'll never understand why some people are so fucked up like that."

"Good......sane people will never understand. Anyway.....I'm going to bed. Goodnight honey. Love you."

"Love you too."

They both kiss each other. Heidi takes her drink and walks upstairs.

Ch. 23

Jackie and Jennifer are in their room with their pajamas on. Jackie takes Abby's journal with her reading glasses and heads downstairs.

Jennifer says, "Hey. I thought you wanted to go to bed."

"Yeah...but I gotta read some of this journal tonight. It belongs to Abby. One of her friends found it and gave it to me."

"Poor girl....I hope that helps you find her."

"I hope so too. Goodnight."

"Goodnight."

Jennifer gets in the bed and turns off the light. Jackie walks downstairs and into the kitchen. She pours herself a glass of cabernet and walks into the living room. She sits on the couch, turns on the lamp, and takes a sip of her wine. She opens Abby's journal.

"Okay Abby. Help me out here."

Ch. 24

Oh my fucking God! It's a bitch being a black woman in America. I mean......shit. women's organizations don't give a fuck about us. I mean when I started at Charm Vault as an HR Intern, all of the new white female employees got a huge ass bouquet of welcoming flowers from the "white girls club" (well except for Kate because she's my BFF and she's dating a black guy) welcoming them to join the Women's Resources Group there or whatever they fucking call it. Meanwhile, I didn't get shit! People always wonder why I don't support women's organizations. Well it's because they're racist as fuck! I mean c'mon! How in the fuck can you say that you support women and yet........when a black woman like myself or any other woman of color comes along for your help....you turn your back on her...and then you expect us to support you when you organize your women's empowerment events. Fuck you bitches! Oh and yet they say that they're having a tough time with equal pay and be like "Oh......not enough of us are in leadership positions...we need more of us." Like....uh yo! At least one of you bitches is up in leadership positions and when you need help, you have your little "white girls club" to lean on. I mean it's bad enough that women of color have to deal with the "Old Boys Club." On top of that shit.......we gotta deal with your "White Girls Club." Y'all have your little women's networking events. Shit.....after my first week here at the company, I went to the Women's Networking Event Charm Vault had in that grand city hall room in the office building. All I saw were white women, talking to all the other young white women professionals. Shit.....I tried striking up a conversation with one of the white female managers there and she just blew me off like she said, "Excuse me. I'll be right back." That bitch left and never came back! I mean one of the very, very few women of color was at a table in the corner. The same damn thing happened to her! I would have sat with Kate but she and Dave went out to dinner for their anniversary.

Ch. 25

My, my, my hahaha. You should've seen the look on that bitch Tammie Trolly's face today when I laid her out! Kate and I were smoking weed on the corporate grounds before we came in for work. That bitch Tammie saw us and walked up to us. She basically scolded us for smoking weed saying, "You two should not be smoking on office grounds! That's against the company's policy!" Hahaha! Guess what I said? I said "Isn't fucking with one of the pharmacists in the lab to get him to make cocaine for you and your two friends against the company's policy too?" Hahahahahahaha! She just stood there with a disgusted look on her face! So then I said, "If you won't tell on us, we won't tell on you. Okay?" Tammie just scrunched her face and stomped off! Hahahahahaha! How classic is that shit?

Ch. 26

Abby's Diary

Ahhhh feminism! Would it be soooo wonderful for us to be treated as good as men? It would be fucking awesome! But........you know that shit is not gonna happen! Why? Because women.....well...........we treat each other like shit! Duh! Here are the following reasons:

-Feminism being elitist (aka not giving a fuck about women of color, women who are members of the LGBT community, women from working class backgrounds or from impoverished upbringings, women who are religious minorities, women with disabilities, etc.)

-A rather unappealing woman seeing an attractive woman and wanting to peel her face off......for just being attractive! C'mon get a fucking grip! Blame your genes for that.....not the woman who's face you want to rip off!

-Female doctors advocating for more female physicians and yet.......they turn around and treat their female patients like shit; ignore their concerns because, like male doctors, female doctors think that women are emotional basket cases that can never be taken seriously.

-Older women bossing younger women around at work. Not to be helpful, but because older women always feel the need to bring young women down to make themselves feel better about their age. Plus I think they've always despised young women anyway.

-Young women completely dismissing helpful suggestions from older women because according to them, all older women have traditional views on feminism and gender roles. Right young ladies.........

(And you know what.......if women didn't treat each other like shit....we would be in a much better position in society; in the workplace or in our households......but......I can't say that because I would be perceived as an asshole. But.....you know I'm right!)

-Working women scolding women who decide to be stay-at-home mothers.

-Stay-at-home mothers scolding mothers who decide to work.

-A woman mistreating another woman for deciding to not have children.

- A woman mistreating another woman for deciding to have children.

-A woman mistreating another woman for deciding to not get married.

--A woman mistreating another woman for deciding to get married.

-Women blaming women for being raped. The summer before I left for college, I volunteered at a hospital. I was just about to leave for the day when I hear this young woman crying while I hear another woman speaking to her. I took a peak in the room and the woman crying looked like she was in her 20s. She had bruises all over her face, arms, and thighs. Her hair was matted. My God! Whoever did that to her deserves a slow and horrible death! The woman speaking was a nurse who looked like she was in her mid 50s. At first, I thought she was comforting her. Well think again.........she was doing the complete opposite. Here's how the conversation went:

The nurse said, "Now honey..........why don't you wear a longer skirt the next time you go out. Okay?"

The girl responded, "But......I thought it was not my fault. I-"

"Hush dear! Maybe if you would respect yourself a little more and dressed more modestly......maybe this would have not happened to you! Now the only type of girl this stuff happens to is the type of girl who has no respect for herself."

"Can I just have the damn rape kit done please?!"

"Oh honey......I'm not going to let you ruin a man's life for your promiscuous ways!"

I walked into the room and said, "Ahhhh.......there's nothing like a nurse blaming yet another woman for being raped! How disgusting!"

I hear someone say, "What is going on here?!"

I turn around and see Dr. Tiffany Gomez and the Head Nurse, Ann, behind me.

I respond, "This nurse refuses to give this poor woman a rape kit."

Dr. Gomez walks over to the patient and softly asks, "Hi. What's your name?"

"Carrie Lever."

"Dr. Gomez continues, "Carrie, is it true that Nurse Jacka Rough, refused to do a rape kit on you when you requested it?"

"Yes! She also blamed me for it! Said that I should dress more modestly! Her reason for not doing the rape kit was because she didn't want me to ruin a man's life for my promiscuous ways!"

Carrie started to cry and Dr. Gomez put a hand on Carrie's shoulder. Then.....Dr. Gomez gives Jacka a dirty look.

Jacka said, "Well.....c'mon! She asked for it!"

Ann said, "Shut up! Come with me Jacka!"

"But-"

"I SAID COME WITH ME!! NOW!"

Jacka scrunched her lips together and left the room.

Dr. Gomez says, "I'll start the rape kit now if that's okay with you."

"Yes that's okay."

"Okay."

As Dr. Gomez gets the kit set up with another nurse......who is much kinder, I'm about to leave when Carrie grabs my hand.

"Can you stay? Please.......I.......can't do this alone......I can't......"

I put my other hand on top of hers, "You are not alone. I'm right here Carrie."

"What do you do here?"

"I'm a volunteer. What do you do?"

"I work at Sterling and Company as an associate. They're an accounting firm."

I nod.

"Uh.....umm......what's your name?"

"Abby."

"Abby.........I didn't do anything wrong.......right?"

"Carrie. You did nothing wrong. You did nothing to deserve this. This is not your fault. Okay?"

"Okay."

"Say it back to me."

"I did nothing wrong. I did nothing to deserve this. This is not my fault."

"Again."

"I did nothing wrong. I did nothing to deserve this. This is not my fault."

"Okay?"

"Okay."

I stayed with her the entire time the rape kit was being done.

Ch. 27

Jackie had Abby's journal on her and fell asleep on the couch. Jennifer walks downstairs.

"Jackie!!"

Jackie wakes up.

"What Jen?"

"Uh.......it's 9am!"

"Oh shit!"

Jackie runs upstairs to get ready for work. She arrives at the station's parking lot.....about an hour later. She gets out of the car and sees Heidi walking in too. Both of them look tired.

"Jackie!"

"Hey! Looks like I'm not the only one running late this morning."

"Jackie.....about yesterday-"

"Don't worry about it. A guy like that would make *anyone* with a conscience go completely nuts."

"Okay."

They walk into the station.

Jackie and Heidi sit at their desks. Tim walks out of his office.

"Jackie, Heidi, in my office now!"

The two ladies look at each other and then walk over to Tim's office. Heidi closes the door and says, "Look Captain....we're sorry we're late."

Tim waved his hand in the air.

"Ehhh....don't worry about it. I got bigger fish to fry anyway. So....is there anything else about the case you wanna mention?"

Jackie said, "I read some of Abby's work journal last night. Her friend, Kate Winger, gave it to me. Abby used to volunteer at a hospital the summer before she attended her first year of college. She stood up for a rape victim who was being given a hard time by one of the nurses there."

"Do you have any names?"

"Yes. The bitch nurse's name is Jacka Rough, the doctor who did the rape kit was Dr. Tiffany Gomez, and the rape victim was Carrie Lever. All of their names were in the journal. She also has an interesting take on *feminism.*"

"How so?"

"She basically criticizes it for being elitist. You know…..excluding women of color, women who are members of the LGBTQ+ community….which frankly I agree with Captain. She also mentioned that the reason why women will never reach full equality is because they treat each other like shit."

"Anything about her co-workers?"

"Besides being excluded from the company's women's programs because of her background….nothing major…….yet. Oh there is one more thing………Tammie Trolly wasn't too fond of Abby and Kate smoking weed on corporate grounds. But then…..Abby knew that Tammie was screwing with one of the pharmacists in the lab to get him to make some cocaine for her and her friends. Can we charge her co-workers with drug use? Oh shit we can't……circumstantial evidence."

"Plus with the company's attorney…….we'd be toast."

Jackie nods.

Tim continues, "Okay…..uh…….track down the doctor who did the rape kit on Carrie Lever, that bitch nurse, and Carrie herself. Also……pay a visit to Charm Vault's corporate office. But tread carefully……the Trolly's are a prominent family here in New Jersey. They do a bunch of fundraisers for good will and do a bunch of things through their foundation or whatever the fuck it's called……okay?"

Both ladies agreed.

"Oh and one more thing Detectives…..do you know what WMLS stands for?"

Heidi says, "No. We're working on it Captain."

Tim nods.

All of the sudden, Charlie Vella, Still Vo's mayor, barges into Tim's office. He looks pissed.

"Tim! What the fuck do you think ya doin'?"

"Charlie-"

"Didn't I tell ya to focus on the garbage can case going on around town?! I got the residents up my ass for this shit!"

"Char-"

"Tim I told ya-"

"SHUT UP!"

Charlie closes his mouth and widens his eyes. Jackie and Heidi are in a corner staring at Charlie.

Tim opens a folder on his desk and spreads out photos of the immigrant kidnapping crime scene at The White's residence. Laid out were photos of starving adults and children....and Angela's bloody crushed skull.

"Look at this shit Charlie! LOOK AT IT! THERE WERE CHILDREN WHO WERE *STARVED* TO DEATH.........AN INNOCENT WOMAN WHO GOT BASHED IN THE HEAD TO DEATH BY SOME BIGOTED BITCH AND YOU WANT ME TO FOCUS ON SOME GODDAMN *GARBAGE CANS?!*"

There was silence in the room for a few seconds then Tim continued.

"THERE WERE 100 PEOPLE DEAD AT THIS CRIME SCENE! DO YOU HEAR ME?! ONE FUCKING HUNDRED! ON TOP OF THAT I GOT A MISSING YOUNG WOMAN THAT WE NEED TO FIND AND *YOUR* PRIORITY IS SOME FUCKING GARBAGE CANS?! HAVE YOU GONE MAD?!"

There is a few seconds of silence and Tim continues.

"MY TOP PRIORITY IS FINDING MS. ABBY BLOCK! THAT IS THE *ONLY* CASE THAT I GIVE A FUCK ABOUT RIGHT NOW!"

A shaking Charlie says, "You.....you know what?"

"WHAT?!"

""Well......well.."

"Am I no longer your Captain Charlie?!"

"Well......you're still captain..."

"THEN GET THE HELL OUT OF HERE SO THAT THESE DETECTIVES CAN GET TO WORK ON THEIR CASE!"

Charlie runs out.

When the door closes, Jackie and Heidi start laughing.

Heidi says, "'About time you put that moron in his place."

A little more settled.....Tim says, "There's only so much shit I can take....including from him."

Jackie and Heidi smile and leave the office. They return to their desks.

Heidi says, "Oh I have to go to the restroom before we go."

"Okay."

As Heidi leaves, Jackie sits down and takes out Abby's journal.

Ch. 28

I just finished reading a magazine. They had a list of the top 5 hospitals in New Jersey. Guess what they all have in common......they are all in predominately white affluent towns. People claim that these suburban neighborhoods have plenty of land and that's why these hospitals are in these neighborhoods and not other neighborhoods.......like urban areas. Well.......that's bullshit. The reason why the top 5 hospitals in New Jersey are in white neighborhoods is because they don't want black people like me.....or any other person of color going to those hospitals because here in America, in order for you to get the best healthcare......you have to be white. Even if you are a person of color who can afford the best healthcare.....you still get pushback from seeking the best care out there. Let me give you a real life example of this shit.

My mother goes to Beacon Health Breast Center at the Beacon Health Ambulatory Care Center out in Little Ville, New Jersey for her annual mammogram and ultrasound. It's no more than 20 minutes away from our home. It is the top breast health center in the state of New Jersey....where like 99% of the staff and physicians are white women. I always go with her each time for moral support. Here's what happened one time we were there. After my mom finished her ultrasound, the technologist left the room. We were there for a few minutes when the radiologist entered the room. Her name was Dr. Geraldine Jean. She has her name on her white coat. She's a white woman that looks to be in her mid 40s. She has thick black glasses on and her hair is up in a messy bun. She has no makeup on........although she could use some. She was cold. She was very distant from us.....didn't even come in talking distance with us. We thought that something was wrong with my mom's results. But then, the cunt began to speak.

"Betty.....that's your name right?"

My mom said, "Uh.......hi. You're name is....?"

"Dr. Jean."

"Well Dr. Jean.......is everything okay with my test results?"

"Yes."

"Okay so.......why are you here?"

"I'm asking the same thing about yourself. How old are you Betty?"

"I'm 55 years old. Why are you asking me?"

"I see that you come here every year. I don't know why because you really don't need a mammogram except if you find a lump."

"Well according to my doctor, I'm supposed to get them annually. Plus the last time I checked.......women my age are recommended to get screening mammograms. So what you're saying doesn't make any sense."

"Well of course it doesn't make any sense to you because you're not a doctor. So do not come here anymore! I don't want to see you anymore!"

My mom had a look of rage that I have never seen on her face........ever. She looked like she wanted to kick this bitch's teeth in. Frankly......that's not such a bad idea.

"Do you give every woman this much of a hard time? Or is it women that look like me that you don't want here in the first place?"

Dr. Jean looked down on the floor and looked up at my mom. She had an uncomfortable look on her face. It went from cold confidence to a still look on her face. Her eyes turned from hazel to black. A chill went up my spine. She left the room......and didn't say a damn word. Hmmmmm......so that's why black women are 40% more likely to die from breast cancer. We see white doctors who don't want to care for us.

My mom's hands were shaking as she got dressed.

"Mom......are you okay?"

She fought back tears as she said, "I'm fine. Let's just get out of here okay Abby?"

When she finished getting dressed I put my hand on her shoulder, "Okay."

As we were leaving the facility, a white woman physician in her 40s approached us. I noticed she approached every woman to find out how their experience was. She was very nice.

"Hi ladies! My name is Dr. Allison Gardner! I'm the director of the Breast Center here! How was your experience today?"

My mom looked at me and gave me a look that said, 'Don't you dare tell her what just happened.'

I said, "Everything was great for my mom....until your racist radiologist who scolded at my mom for getting her annual mammogram."

Dr. Gardner covered her mouth, "Oh my God. I'm.......I'm so very sorry."

I said, "Sorry.......wow! Why did you hire her?"

"The old director must have hired her. I just started here two weeks ago."

"Oh.......um......I'm sorry."

"Don't be. You didn't know."

Dr. Gardner walked over to a black woman doctor in her 40s, and whispered in her ear. Both of them walked over to us. Dr. Gardner walked us into a private room and continued. It's the first time I saw a black doctor here at the center.

"This is Dr. Candice Miller. She will be reading your scans Dr. Jean went over. Okay?"

"Okay," my mother said.

While Dr. Miller led us to the exam room, I saw Dr. Gardner talking to Dr. Jean. She said,

"Dr. Jean. I need to see you in my office now."

"Are you kidding me-"

"I said now!"

Dr. Jean looked at my mom and I. I raise my eyebrow and shook my head.

Luckily, my mom's scans came out okay.

Let me give you another example. I went to an OB/GYN some time ago. Her name was Dr. Tess Trick. I went there for my annual checkup. My other OB/GYN, who was awesome, retired so I had to find a new one. The staff was of course all white. I was called into the exam room and the medical assistant, who was quite distant, took my vitals.

The medical assistant asked, "Are you pregnant?"

"No I'm not pregnant."

She looked at me for a few seconds.

"What?"

She picked up her folder and said, "Take everything off, put the gown on with the opening in the front. Dr. Trick will be here in a few."

She closed the door and I got undressed and put on the gown.

I here a knock on the door.

I say, "Yes?"

Dr. Trick entered the room. She was a white woman in her 50s. She had a white coat on with black hair down to her shoulders. She, like the medical assistant, was also very distant. She didn't shake my hand. She just simply stood by the door and crossed her arms across her chest.

"So.....when was your last gynecologic exam?"

"Uh......hi Dr. Trick. I'm good how are you?"

"Don't get smart with me young lady."

"What's wrong with being smart?"

She just looked at me.

"Okay......my last exam was last year. Why?"

"Because you really don't need gynecologic exams unless you have a problem."

"Really.....?"

"Don't question me. I'm the doctor. You're the patient. So are sure you're not pregnant?"

"What makes you think I'm not sure?"

Dr. Trick just stands there.

"Do you give every woman this much of a hard time? Or are there certain women you don't want coming here at all?"

Dr. Trick's lips start to scrunch.

"Okay.....lean back on the table."

"No I'm not going to do that.........especially since I know what kind of person you are."

She took a deep breath and walked out of the room.

Hmmmmmm........so that's why black women are more likely to die from pregnancy.

You know........Evan and I casually talked about having kids one day after we get married. He seemed so excited and I pretended to be excited. But actually....I'm terrified at the thought of being pregnant. What if I come across a doctor like Dr. Trick who looks at me as another black woman that she doesn't care about. My worse nightmare is pregnant me lying on the bed getting ready to deliver my baby. The all white medical staff there rolling their eyes thinking, 'Oh...another one of them is having kids...and she's having them with a guy like him.....just great.' I'm complaining that I feel lightheaded and something is not right. The doctor just tells me to 'suck it up. I'm having a baby.' When I push, I start to scream. The doctor tells me to 'stop being so dramatic. It can't hurt that bad.' I push and scream again and the doctor rolls her eyes. My baby comes out fine and healthy. It's a girl! But then I start slipping away. I bleed out to death and the medical staff treats my black body as a duffle bag they want to get rid of. The way they treat Evan is just absolutely awful. Not comforting him at all as he's crying and holding my baby.........my sweet baby who will be raised without her mother. One of the nurses tells him that he only has a minute because they have to get rid of my body for the next woman to come in and deliver her baby. As Evan walks over to me crying, the doctor tells a nurse, "I hope he finds a woman more suitable to have a child." Evan wants to be a father. My parents want to become grandparents. I want to be a mother. However......I don't want my parents to bury their only child. I don't want Evan to bury his wife and raise our child on his own. I don't want to leave my child without their mother to raise them....hug them.......comfort them when they're feeling down and say that everything will be okay. A black woman with a graduate degree is more likely to die from child-birth than a white woman who didn't finish high school. I want to be a mother......but I don't want to be a statistic either.

Jackie closes the journal as she sees Heidi walking towards her.

"Ready Jackie?"

"I want to ask the Captain if we could question a few more people."

"Okay."

The ladies enter Tim's office.

Jackie says, "Captain. I read some more of Abby's journal. Dr. Geraldine Jean who works at the Beacon Health Breast Center discriminated against Abby's mom because she was black. Abby notified Dr. Allison Gardner, the director there, and she had Dr. Candice Miller review Abby's mother's scans. The scans came back fine. Then Abby went to Dr. Tess Trick for a checkup. Dr. Trick gave her a hard time because she was black. I was thinking of tracking them all down...if that's okay with you."

"Absolutely! For this case ladies…..moving forward, whoever you feel the need to question go ahead and do it. I want this case solved as soon as possible. Those initials that the White's had on their bulletin board……I think they might be connected to Abby's disappearance. If it is……….I want her found sooner……rather than later. Okay?"

They both agreed.

As the ladies left the building and got in the car, Heidi went over the initials and Jackie is on her phone.

"WMLS, WMLS, WMLS……..what the hell could that possibly mean?"

"I don't know. It's driving me crazy!! Anyway I looked up Dr. Allison Gardner. She's now the Director of the Breast Center at Taylor-Conner Medical Center in Wake View, New Jersey."

"That's just 20 minutes away from here.

"Oh……Dr. Candice Miller is also the Director of Breast Radiology there too."

"Umm……interesting. Well…..let's go!"

Ch. 29

The Detectives arrive at Taylor-Conner Medical Center. They walk straight to the Breast Center there and ask the receptionist for Dr. Allison Gardner. The center's medical staff is all women but it's racially diverse. Within a few minutes, Dr. Gardner arrives and shakes their hands.

"Hi Detectives. Pleasure meeting you; let's go into my office for more privacy."

The detectives nod.

They enter into her office. It looks like a typical doctor's office. It has a stained brown wooden desk with a black leather chair and two green cushion chairs on the other side. Across the office, there is a small round wooden table with four green cushion chairs. The floor is hard wood. Dr. Gardner has pictures on her desk of her husband and two children about high school aged.

They hear a knock on the door.

Allison says, "Come in."

Dr. Candice Miller enters.

"Oh Detectives. I hope you don't mind if Dr. Candice Miller is here with us."

Heidi says, "Not a problem! By the way Dr. Miller, you saved us the trip!"

They all laugh.

They all sit at the round table.

Candice says, "So Detectives....you're here to ask about Abby Block right?

Jackie says, "Yes."

"Terrible....I hope you find her."

"Me too. So Detective Smith and I found out that Abby Block and her mother, Betty came to the Beacon Health Breast Center some time ago for Betty's annual mammogram. We know that Dr. Geraldine Jean discriminated against Betty because she was black."

Heidi says, "We know that Abby brought it to your attention Dr. Gardner and you Dr. Miller reviewed Betty's scans Do we have that right?"

Both doctors nodded.

Jackie asks, "So Dr. Gardner.....what did you do with Dr. Jean.?"

"I took her into my office and fired her."

Candice jumps in, "I was the only black doctor there. Allison was the one who hire me. We went to the same medical school. We met at an alumni event and the rest is history. Anyway.....I'm going off topic. Uh.....Dr. Jean gave me a lot of issues too. She wouldn't talk to me, ever."

Allison looked down at her hands with an annoyed look on her face.

Heidi said, "You okay?"

She looked back up, "The same day I fired Geraldine.......I was fired too."

Heidi said, "What?!"

"Geraldine's father is the Chief Medical Officer for the whole Beacon Healthcare System."

"The same day Allison was fired....I quit."

"Then I was hired by Dr. Jill Taylor, one of the founders of Taylor-Conner Medical Center and I hired Candice to come with me."

Heidi said, "You two seem happy here."

Candice said, "Drs. Jill Taylor and Jane Conner founded this medical center because they were fed up about going to top quality medical centers that had no diversity. So far, the hospital has been doing well. Last year, they just made the top five hospitals in New Jersey in the 5th spot. Everyone is so nice here. This is the only place where I feel.....safe. Where people care about what skills you bring to the table.....not whether you're male or female, black or white."

Allison said, "They don't put up with any crap either. Some time ago, a rape victim was here....and this is when the hospital had *just* opened. A nurse, Jacka Rough, was fired for giving a rape victim a hard time."

Heidi and Jackie looked at each other.

Allison asked, "What's going on Detectives?"

Jackie says, "We know you can't give us the name of the victim. But....was a Dr. Tiffany Gomez and a Head Nurse Ann there?"

Allison said, "Yes. They were incredible. The Head Nurse Ann is Tiffany's mother. Tiffany was the one who created the Dr. Gomez Sexual Assault Survivor Center here after she did the rape kit for the victim that day. She's still the director there and her mother is the head nurse there too."

Jackie asks, "Do you know where we could possibly find Jacka Rough?

Allison says, "We really don't know. But Dr. Gomez would certainly be able to help you with that."

Heidi says, "Great. That helps us a lot. We need to pay her a visit too."

Jackie asks, "Do you two know anything about Dr. Tess Trick?"

Candice said, "Yes. I tried reporting her to the state medical board but......."

"But what?"

"Her father is the CEO of Beacon Healthcare System. He knows a lot of people on the state medical board. When I put in the complaint, it got pushed under the rug faster than you can put someone under general anesthesia."

"Damn."

Candice looks at her watch, "Sorry Detectives. I have to go. I have a core needle biopsy procedure to do."

Allison says, "I'm seeing a patient in a few."

Heidi says, "Thank you so much for helping us."

Candice, "Of course. Good luck to you both."

Jackie says, "Thank you."

The Detectives arrive at the Dr. Gomez Sexual Assault Survivor Center and went to the receptionist to ask for Dr. Tiffany Gomez. Within a few minutes, Tiffany and her mother, Ann, walk towards them.

Tiffany says, "Hi Detectives. Please come on back."

The four of them went back to Tiffany's office. It looked very similar to Allison's office with pictures of her family on the desk.

Tiffany asks, "So what can I help you with?"

Heidi said, "Detectives Barns and I are working on the Abby Block case. Did she volunteer here the summer before she started college?"

Tiffany says, "Yes she did volunteer here once. She was one of the best ones we've had. She's such a wonderful person. It's terrible what happened to her. At the end of her time here with us, I asked her if she thought about becoming a psychologist. She didn't seem to be that interested in pursuing the profession. But I still told her to think about it."

Jackie asks, "Can you tell us what happened to Jacka Rough?"

Ann said, "Last I heard, she died of cancer last year. It was a slow and painful death for her. I'm glad it was."

"Mom?!"

"Oh I hated the bitch! She was soooooo nasty to the patients, especially towards the women!"

Tiffany looks at her watch and says, "Is there anything else we can do for you Detectives? Sorry to be in such a rush but we have a new patient coming in."

Jackie says, "No not a problem. I think what you're doing here is wonderful for the survivors."

"Thanks. I couldn't have done it without Dr. Jill Taylor and Dr. Jane Connor. The minute I told them about creating this center, they gave me the nod and told me to run with it. I owe those two incredible women everything."

Ann says, "Dr. Taylor is African American and Dr. Connor is a lesbian. They're around my age so you can imagine how much shit they had to put up with when they were up and coming."

Heidi says, "I'm sure. Thank you."

Tiffany says, "Of course and good luck."

Jackie says, "Thanks."

Ch. 30

Heidi and Jackie arrive at Dr. Tess Trick's practice. When they get there, they see the receptionist. In a few minutes Dr. Tess Trick walks up....along with Dr. Geraldine Jean. The Detectives look shocked.

Heidi said, "Hi doctors."

Tess said, "Hi Detective....this way please."

"The four of them walk through the door and stop in the hallway."

Tess says to Jackie, "Oh young lady....you have to wait outside for someone to call you in."

"I'm Detective Smith's partner Detective Barns."

"Oh....well......what can I do for you both?"

Heidi says, "We're working on the Abby Block case."

"Okay."

Heidi and Jackie look at each other.

"We are aware that Abby came here some years ago for her annual checkup. You Dr. Trick gave her a hard time for being here."

Jackie jumps in, "And you Dr. Jean gave Abby's mother a hard time for coming to Beacon Health Breast Center for her annual mammogram."

"Hey Jackie....do you know what these situations have in common?"

"Yeah Heidi.......they didn't want people that look like me to come to their offices for medical care."

Both doctors had stone cold looks on their faces.

A blond woman with a blouse and slacks came out into the hallway from the waiting area.

She said, Tess......Geraldine......is everything okay?"

She looks at the Detectives.

"And who are you ladies?"

Heidi says, "I'm Detective Smith. This is my partner Detective Barns. Who are you?"

"I'm Kristen Graves, Dr. Trick and Dr. Jean's attorney."

Geraldine said, "They're here about the Abby Block case."

"Which my clients have nothing to do with."

Jackie asks, "Dr. Jean.....what are you doing here?"

Tess said, "Dr. Jean here is a friend as well as a *patient* of mine."

"My God...... Jackie what do you call two bigots that come together to do something?"

"A *klan*tastrophy."

Kristen says, "Okay Detectives I'm going to have to ask you to leave. We're done answering questions."

Heidi and Jackie look at each other and walk away.

They get into the car.

Heidi says, "What the *hell* was *that*?"

Jackie says, "I'm asking you the same question."

"Wanna visit Carrie Lever?"

"Sure."

"You said that she has her own accounting firm right?"

"Yeah......guess where it is?"

"No way Jackie."

"Yep right in Still Vo."

"Small world."

"It sure is."

They arrive at a corporate office complex and locate Carrie's office on the fifth floor. When they enter the lobby, they see Carrie speaking with a client. When the client leaves, Carrie walks over to them and shakes their hands.

"Hi ladies! Can I help you?"

"I'm Detective Barns and this is my partner Detective Smith."

"Oh um.....what can I do for you Detectives?"

"We're investigating the Abby Block case and wanted to ask you a few questions about Abby. Is that okay?"

"Of course. Let's go into my office."

They walk into her office. Her office has the standard wooden desk with a black leather chair and two black cushion chairs on the other side. She has pictures of her husband and her son and daughter on it. She also has a small rectangular table with six chairs around it. The window shows a beautiful view of the gardens surrounding the office.

Jackie says, "You have a beautiful family Carrie."

"Thank you! That's my husband Stewart, my son Jake and my daughter Tina!"

Heidi says, "Looks like your accounting practice has grown!"

"Yes it has! I now have 50 employees! It's the best decision I ever made!"

Jackie, "So Carrie-"

"Oh are you hear about the Abby Block case?!"

"Yes Carrie we-"

"That's horrible what happened to that girl!"

"Carrie......."

Carrie starts to cry, "You two know how Abby and I crossed paths don't you?"

Jackie and Heidi look at each other.

Jackie continues, "We........we were wondering what Abby is like...personality wise."

"She is a great person. She helped me get through the most humiliating time of my life. She made the rape kit easier to endure. That kit felt like......like........I was being *hurt* again but......I wanted the bastard that did that to me locked up! I'm so glad he's in prison! I never felt safe between the time I was raped and the day of sentencing. People say that survivors like myself eventually get over it........we never do. We get better at dealing with what happened to us but......we never forget the most humiliating time of our lives. The best thing Abby has done for me was to let me know that this was not my fault. Just after it happened......I kept thinking what if I did this, what if I did that, what did I do to deserve this. But she reminded me *I did nothing wrong. I did nothing to deserve this. This is not my fault.* Every time I even got the thought in my head that it was my fault.....I would say those three thoughts to myself.......I still have to do that every now and then. My therapist said that it was great Abby gave me something to say to myself whenever I started blaming myself."

Jackie and Heidi nod.

"I hope that helps."

Heidi says, "Yes it does Carrie. Thank you."

Carrie looks at her phone, "Oh I have a prospective client coming in about ten minutes. So sorry to cut this short ladies."

She gets up with her makeup bag, opens her closet across from her office, and looks in the mirror. Heidi takes a few tissues from her tissue box and gives them to Carrie.

"Oh thank you."

She dabs her eyes and reapplies her mascara and lipstick.

"Okay ladies.....how do I look?"

Jackie says, "You look great."

"Thanks."

"Don't worry....we can see ourselves out."

"Are you ladies sure?"

"Yes."

Carrie reaches out and hugs them at the same time.

"You detectives will find her. You two seem like you really care about this case. We need more people like that in the world."

Heidi and Jackie agreed.

The detectives got in their car.

Jackie says, "God.....I really hate bringing up that terrible night to sexual assault survivors."

"Me too.......but we had to do it."

"I know........at least it helps us get a well rounded view of what Abby's like. She seems to be a good person that just doesn't understand why people do such horrible things to others for no reason."

"Isn't that all of us?"

"Um.....kind of."

"Okay Jackie.......what's up?"

"Look.....I just wanna find this kid."

"Me too Jackie. Me too."

"Should we pay a visit to Kate Winger?"

"It's the afternoon so everybody should be at lunch by now at Charm Vault."

"Okay then."

They arrive at Charm Vault's offices. They see Kate outside in the courtyard eating a whole pizza pie with a bottle of soda. The detectives walk over to her.

Jackie says, "Hi Kate! Oh......is that pizza?!"

Kate says, "Yeah!"

Heidi says nodding at the pizza, "You're waiting for someone?"

"I'm waiting for Abby."

Jackie said, "Kate.....Abby isn't here......is everything okay?"

Kate slams down her pizza slice and starts to cry.

Heidi and Jackie sit next to her on each side. Jackie puts her arm around her.

"All I do is *eat* and *drink*.....and *eat* some more. I mean shit! I gained 10 pounds since Abby's gone missing. I try talking to my parents but with their old school southern charm they tell me I have to suck it up...for Abby. My boyfriend tries to help but.....he can only do but so much. I eat practically all day and when I get home I drink myself to sleep. I feel so alone without her. She's my right hand.....what can I do without my right hand?!"

Kate continues crying. Heidi holds Kate's hand. She gently says, "Kate......have you thought about talking to someone.....a therapist maybe?"

Kate leaves Jackie's arms, let's go of Heidi's hand, and stands up to face them.

"Oh no. No, no, no, no, no! I.....I can't speak to a shrink. There's no *way* I could do that!"

Heidi says, "Kate......you told us that you *drink* yourself to sleep. That's not good."

Jackie jumps in, "That's not healthy. You can't carry on like this."

Kate puts her hand on her head, "Okay....I'll think about."

Heidi asks, "Is Tammie Trolly here?"

"No. She's taking a day off."

"Um......perks of being the company founder's granddaughter huh?"

"Yep....and many more perks that come with that."

"Like what?"

"She comes in two hours late sometimes, gives Abby, Becca, Lena, and I a *really* hard time all the time."

"Why?"

"Does Abby being black, Becca McCluster being gay, Alice Rodriguez being Latina, and me having a black boyfriend ring a bell to you?"

Jackie and Heidi look at each other.

Jackie says, "Can you be more specific?"

"Well for starters we're never invited to her mansion for the informal HR get-togethers and she makes us feel unwelcomed at the company's women's events. You know stuff like that."

Heidi says, "Have you told your boss, the Head of HR, about it?"

Kate chuckles, "You're kidding me right? The company is more conservative than the majority of the residents of Still Vo. In corporate, you don't report it...you just deal with it."

"Yeah but......companies are obligated to help their minority employees feel safe at work free of discrimination."

"If they actually cared......corporate would be way more diverse than it is now. Things haven't changed much since Danielle became head of the department. After all....the Trolly family runs the company....not her."

Heidi just looked at her.

"Uh.....who are you two?"

The three ladies look around and see Danielle approach them.

Jackie says, "I'm Detective Barns and this is my partner Detective Smith. We're working on Abby's case."

"Oh.........sorry about that."

Jackie says, "It's cool."

Kate says, "Sorry to cut this short but..........I gotta go and get some work done. Oh and by the way.......feel free to take some pizza...."

Heidi said, "Thanks."

As Kate leaves, Jackie starts to speak.

"So Danielle.....Kate told us a little more about Tammie Trolly."

Danielle says, "Yeah......"

"Care to tell us more?"

Danielle takes a deep breath, "Look........when I interviewed for the job, they were impressed with the Diversity and Inclusion program I implemented at my last employer. I wasn't dying to leave but Charm Vault offered me a larger salary than the one I had at the time so I accepted the offer. However, when I started here...things were different. I started bringing in more diverse candidates for various roles here. Every time when I brought in a highly qualified candidate that wasn't white.....the hiring managers started grilling them....asking them questions that had *nothing* to do with the job itself. When I asked them why they didn't hire them.....they said it was because they weren't the right *organizational fit.* When I hired Kate for the HR internship program...I had no trouble. I started getting a lot of shit for hiring Kate when the company found out that her boyfriend was black. That was several weeks after she started. But when it came to hiring Abby, Becca, and Alice for the HR internship program......I got a lot of pushback. They didn't want to hire them at all. I've reached my breaking point then because these three ladies were extremely talented. But when I asked them was it because they weren't considered all American girls to them......that's when they *reluctantly* hired them. Abby was the one who helped me a lot with putting the company's Human Resources Leadership Development Program together. It was her idea to start the program. One day, the CEO, Tom Trolly, came into my office to tell me that the program has been approved, I told him that I couldn't have done it without Abby. His face turned from a smile to a frown and he walked out of my office. Abby, Kate, Alice, and Becca came to me because they felt like Tammie Trolly was excluding them from the company's women's initiatives. I brought Tammie into my office to ask her about it. She had the nerve to tell me they weren't interested in participating in any of the women's initiatives. I told her that I know that was a lie and gave her a verbal warning. The next thing I knew....I was being yelled at by Tom Trolly in his office for giving his daughter such a hard time and if I ever did that again I would be looking for a new job. He also said that filing a complaint wouldn't do me any good because he's good friends with the governor of New Jersey, the County Executive, and several judges and that he would be able to sweep the complaint under the rug. He also told me that if I kept pushing my *diversity bullshit* on this company....same consequence applies. So....I just lay low."

Heidi said, "It seems like you're miserable here. Why can't you just leave?"

"My husband and I divorced last year. He married the 21 year old he cheated on me with. My son is in college and my daughter who's in high school has just been diagnosed with autism. My ex-husband pays for child support and I got something from the divorce. But I still need the paycheck to put my son through college and the health insurance to cover my daughter's medical expenses. So I need to keep this job."

"Sorry to hear that."

"Thanks."

"So why are you telling us all of this."

"Well first off......*I didn't tell you any of this*. Secondly......I think Tammie had something to do with Abby's disappearance. Like what happened to Becca and Alice."

Heidi and Jackie look at each other. Jackie asks, "Becca and Alice are missing? For how long?"

"For about over a year now.....the two of them lived in Broomville, NJ, where The Trolly's live. That family has that police department wrapped around their fingers. They didn't even thoroughly investigate their disappearances. They questioned a few people and just put it on hold. I'm pretty sure the Trolly's paid them off to do so. The case was never solved. Tammie hated them *a lot*. They went missing just a week after I offered them to come back for the HRLD program after they graduated from grad school. I gave them the news just before they were scheduled to go back to school for the fall semester. She hated Abby too and now she's missing........something's not right about this company."

Jackie takes a deep breath, "Wow.........Danielle........thanks. This helps us *a lot*."

"I'm glad it did. I'm surprised that you detectives are taking a risk to get Abby's case solved."

Heidi asks, "What are you insinuating?"

"The Trolly's have *a shit load* of influence in New Jersey. Having their company, which is the top pharmaceutical company in the world, being headquartered in this state.....benefits *a lot* of higher-ups in the state financially. The Trolly's are a prominent family in New Jersey. They know *a lot* of important people and have enough money to pay people off to look away from their wrongdoings. Look if I were you.......be careful. Do you have families?"

The detectives nod.

"Just be careful okay......for your families' sake."

Heidi asks, "If you're so scared of them....why are you telling us all of this?"

"Because I can only sit back for so long and continue to let people abuse others......and you ladies seem like you care about doing the right thing. Oh and like I said earlier.......*I did not tell you any of this*."

They both say, "Tell us what?"

The three ladies give each other a smirk.

Jackie says, "Oh......do you mind if Heidi and I take the pizza?"

"Oh no go ahead."

"Thanks."

Ch. 31

Heidi and Jackie return to the police department. Tim calls them into his office. They see Derek Hunting, the County Executive of Mullville County.........which includes the towns Still Vo and Broomville. Derek begins to speak.

"Look I want everyone here to layoff the Trolly family. They are great citizens of this county. They have contributed greatly to our community and I don't want to fuck that up! In fact......I want all of you to put the Abby Block case on hold. It seems like none of you are gettin' anywhere. So that shouldn't be a problem right?"

Jackie and Heidi look at Tim.

Tim says, "Sure Derek. In fact.......Jackie and Heidi are taking a vacation starting tomorrow. They haven't taken a vacation in a long, long time. They already put in their request!"

"Oh wonderful! Ladies! Enjoy your time with your families!"

They both said, "Thank you."

"Okay well I gotta go! Good talk Tim!"

"Likewise."

As Derek leaves, Jackie closes the door, "Captain....what the *hell* just happened?!"

"You and Heidi are *officially* off the Abby Block case."

Heidi said, "Oh c'mon Captain! Really?"

"This is crazy!"

"You ladies didn't hear me. I said you two are *officially* off the Abby Block case."

The ladies look at each other.

"Why the hell do you two think I told the County Exec that you were going to be on vacation starting tomorrow?"

Jackie shakes her head, "Wait....so let me get this straight....you want Heidi and I to work on this case......*unofficially?*"

"Look......if you work on this case officially, you'll won't get anywhere. If you work on it unofficially......no one will suspect you. Hey....someone might give you two a major lead."

"Captain.....what if people find out we're on the case about this....*unofficially?*"

"You let me worry about that."

Heidi said, "Captain......are you sure?"

"Yes. You two are following your Captain's orders. That's all you're doing."

Jackie says, "The County Exec is a good friend of the Trolly family."

Heidi says, "You mean he's a good bitch of the Trolly family."

Jackie chuckles and continues.

"The family is well connected......the governor of New Jersey is a good friend of theirs....so are a few judges. They're total bigots. They treated Abby terribly. A couple of the employees of the HR department there, where Tammie also is, have gone missing. One is Latina the other one is a lesbian."

Tim widens his eyes, "Wait.......what? What are their names?"

"Becca McCluster and Alice Rodriguez."

"Oh my God...what town did they live in?"

"Broomville.....where also the Trolly family lives."

"*Broomville*.........enough said. The cops in that town act like they are hired by the Trolly's instead of the town. How about those doctors you talked too?"

Heidi says, "Nothing that was extremely helpful. We even talked to the rape victim Abby helped when she was volunteering at the hospital. Oh.....hear this.......the racists radiologist that discriminated against Abby's mom is a patient of the ob/gyn that discriminated against Abby, Dr. Tess Trick. We tried asking them questions but....their attorney was there....."

Tim asks, "How about the initials WMLS?"

"Still nothing."

Tim takes a deep breath, "I find it strange how the County Executive wants us off the Abby case. Not that I think he has something to do with it but.......I think he knows something about it....and that the Trolly's have a connection to it. Look.........tread *carefully*.........and get this case solved...okay?"

They both agreed.

Ch. 32

Jackie and Heidi visit the Block residence the following morning.

Heidi says, "It's sure nice to be wearing jeans instead of that damn pantsuit all the time."

"Girl I'm right here with you."

Betty opens the door and leads them to the living room.

"My husband is still asleep. Would you ladies like something to drink? Coffee? Tea?"

Heidi says, "Coffee sounds great."

Jackie says, "Same here."

Betty leaves for a few and returns with a tray with three mugs on it each filled with coffee. She sets it on the table and sits on the couch across from the detectives.

Jackie says, "We would ask how you and your husband are feeling but.....I know you're not feeling well at all."

"Thanks for that Jackie."

Betty begins to look frustrated and continues.

"So.......I heard that the town has put Abby's case on hold.....care to tell me what the hell is going on here? Oh! Did you two come *all* the way over here to tell me *that?!*"

The detectives look at each other.

Jackie says, "No Betty......we came here to tell you that.....Heidi, our captain, and I are still working on the case.....*unofficially.*"

"Is.......is that even ethical?"

"Technically....no. But since the County Executive wants to play dirty.......might as well get in the mud with them....right?"

Betty nods.

Heidi says, "I see the signs still up around town."

"Yeah....that didn't do shit! I just.....I just want my daughter here! I want her here.....with me....with her father....with her boyfriend......with her friends....with people that care about her! I don't give a flying *fuck* what you ladies have to do to find my daughter! I don't care if you have to *pull* some strings to do it! Just find Abby! Please!"

Jackie leans forward on her knees, "We're *going* to find her."

Heidi also leans forward on her knees, "You have our word."

Betty looks down at her hands and looks up, "Good. Now stop trying to comfort me here and go find my Abby!"

Ch. 33

Evan wakes up in the morning in his apartment in NYC. He smells coffee brewing. He gets out of bed and walks into the kitchen with just his boxers on. He sees Abby pouring coffee in two mugs and gives one to Evan. She has nothing but a bra and panties on. Both of them are white lace. Evan *always* gets hot when she wears that…..makes him want to peel them right off of her and make her happy inside. They both put cream and sugar in their coffee and take a sip. Abby begins to speak.

"How's your coffee?"

"It's great as always. But not as good as the way you make me feel when we have fun………..all………day………..long."

They waste no time. Evan walks over to Abby and kisses her for a long time. Abby puts her hand down his boxers and feels his package. Evan starts to breath hard.

She says, "You want me to make you happy?"

"Yes Abby….very…..very much."

"Come."

With her hand still in his boxers, they walk into the bedroom. He takes her hand out of his boxers.

"Take that lace off. Let me see the rest of you."

She unhooks her bra and throws it to the side. She takes off her panties and lets them fall to her ankles. She steps out of them. He picks her up and kisses her again. He kisses her breasts and she starts breathing hard. He throws her onto the bed and slips his boxers off. He crawls on top of her…….with his package ready to go. He kisses her and his hand starts rubbing up and down between her legs. Her hips move to the same beat as his hand. Evan feels that Abby is wet……and ready to go too. He enters her and glides in and out. They continue to kiss. Abby starts to feel a tingle spreading throughout her hips and she starts to moan. Evan moves faster and Abby reaches her peak…..screaming pleasure that is caused by her good feelings. While Abby is still screaming pleasure…..Evan reaches his peak and he starts screaming pleasure. When they are done……they look at each other and kiss. They stop and Evan looks at her.

"This outfit looks good on you."

"I like your outfit too."

They start laughing. Not long after.....they fuck again in bed......then on the living room couch.......then on the kitchen counter........then.....everywhere else. When they are done.......they return back to bed, have sex again.....and then they just lay together facing each other.

"I love you Evan."

"I love you too Abby."

She smiles at him.

He smiles at her.

———

Evan hears his phone ring. He wakes up and doesn't find Abby next to him. It was a dream. He had a dream of sharing a beautiful moment with Abby.....and the kinds of sex they have had on a regular basis. He gets up and answers his cell. It's Jane Pale....Evan's mom.

"Hello?"

"Evan? Honey it's 12:15 in the afternoon!"

"Mom.......I'm taking off today."

"I know! That's why I'm calling you! Can you get over here in Broomville? Your father and I are going to be at the Broomville Country Club in a little bit. We would love it if you would come! Plus.....we have a big surprise for you!"

Evan takes a deep breath, "Okay Mom. I'll be there soon. Bye."

He hangs up.

Big surprise?! Maybe they're giving him the company to run! That would be awesome!

Evan gets out of bed and gets ready for the day.

Ch. 34

When Evan enters the country club, he sees his parents sitting at the table. He notices that a family of three is sitting at the same table.

His mom sees him, "Hi Evan! Glad you could make it! Have a seat."

Evan sits between his parents. Sitting across from him is a beautiful young white woman about Abby's age. She is also sitting between her parents. Evan's mom continues speaking.

"Evan this is Isabelle and her parent's Jack and Samantha Trope."

Evan shakes hands with all three of them.

His mom says, "We met them a few weeks ago. They just moved to Broomville. They own the Trope Investment firm in NYC. It was founded by Jack's grandfather.

Evan says, "Cool."

Samantha says, "Oh and Evan....Isabelle here is single!"

Isabelle says, "Mom?!"

Jane says, "Oh! Evan is single too!"

Evan glares at his mom and she continues.

"He's been single for some time now! Isabelle and him should spend some time together! I-"

"Sorry for the confusion but......I actually *have* a girlfriend."

The Trope family looks at Jane.

Jane says, "Excuse us for one second."

Evan says, "Sorry.......excuse us."

Jane and Evan walk outside into the courtyard.

"Mom?! What are you doing?!"

"I'm trying to get you with a young woman that is more on your level......and more tasteful! It was very rude of you to just cut me off like that while I was talking to them! Isabelle has good pedigree! Now since that Abby girl is gone........you need to move on! Hey! Look at this as a second chance to date the *right* woman!"

Evan puts his hands on his head and walks back and forth.

"Are you serious Mom?! Wow! Just........wow! Mom......this isn't right!"

"If you knew what was *right* you wouldn't be with someone like Abby in the *goddamn first place!*"

Evan puts his hands down and gives her a strong glare.

Jane takes a deep breath and puts her hand on Evan's shoulder, "Hon-"

Evan shrugs her hand off, "Get off of me!"

"Evan-"

"Did *you* take her?"

"What? Evan-"

"DID YOU TAKE HER MOM?! DID YOU KIDNAP ABBY?!"

"Oh Evan! Don't be ridiculous! I would *never* do something like that! You *know* that I would never do something like that!"

"You know what Mom..........after that shit you just-"

"Watch your language young man!"

"SHUT UP!!"

Jane jumps and puts her hand on her mouth.

"After that *shit* you just pulled in there.......I don't even *know* you anymore!"

Jim Pale enters the courtyard and approaches the two.

"What the *hell* is going on here?"

"Dad......are you fucking kidding me?! You know exactly what's going on here! Mom trying to set me up with another woman while Abby is still missing! Have you two gone completely MAD?!"

Jim slaps Evan's face hard. He puts his finger in Evan's face.

"Now you *know* better than to speak to your mom and I like that young man! We're trying to help you stay on the right path and that Abby was steering you the wrong way! YOU OUTTA BE ASHAMED-"

Evan pushes his father hard and Jim falls to the ground. Jane runs to him and kneels next to him.

"You're damn right Dad! I am ashamed! *I am ashamed to be your son!*"

Evan starts walking away.

Jim yells at him.

"Evan! Evan! Get back here right now! Evan!"

He ignores his dad's command.

Ch. 35

Jackie and Heidi enter Broomville. They first stop at Alice Rodriguez's parents' mansion. They knock on the door and Nina Rodriguez, her mother, opens it.

"Hi ladies. Can I help you with something?"

Jackie says, "Hi Mrs. Rodriguez. I'm Detective Smith this is my partner Detective Barns-"

"Oh you're here about Abby Block right? The girl who's missing?"

They nod.

"You know....she works for the same company that Alice works for...uh...Charm Vault Pharmaceuticals. Oh sorry to keep you two out here. Please come in!"

They step into her house. The foyer is long with a marble floor. The living room and foyer are painted in light blue. The plush couches are also light blue and so is the carpet. There is a glass coffee table in the center.

"Would you two like anything to drink?"

They both say, "No thank you."

"My husband, Rafael, is at work. He's an investment banker in the city. Please sit."

The detectives sit on one couch and Nina sits on the couch across from them.

"I thought that Abby's case was put on hold by the County Executive."

Heidi says, "Like he did for Alice's case......right?"

Nina looks down at her hands, "That bastard! It didn't make much of a difference anyway!"

She looks up and continues, "The cops here didn't do shit to find my daughter!"

Jackie asks, "Can you tell us how the investigation went?"

"Oh....it was a *fucking joke* to them! They didn't question *anyone* except for Rafael and I! *When did we last see her?* and *Was she promiscuous?* Because everyone thinks that Latinas have sex with *everyone*! We suspected that the Trolly family had something to do with it! Alice told me about the way that bitch Tammie treated her!"

Heidi asks, "What did Alice tell you about Tammie?"

"She kept asking Alice if she was *sure* she was born here? That she didn't want to sit near Alice because she was afraid of the germs that she got from Mexico."

Nina started to cry, "I know......I know Tammie had *something* to do with Alice's disappearance. I mean Alice going missing when she just got offered to join the company full time when she graduated? I mean......I can't think of anyone else that would want to hurt my only child!"

Heidi said, "Mrs. Rodriguez......this investigation will be different. We're going to do *everything* in our power to find Alice. You have my word."

Jackie said, "You have my word too."

"I thought my Alice's case was put on hold....and so was Abby's."

Heidi says, "*Officially*.......yes is it. *Unofficially*.......we're not done until these cases are *solved*."

Nina nodded and the doorbell rings.

"Excuse me ladies."

Nina gets up and walks to the door. A middle-aged woman enters the house.

"Detectives, this is Donna McCluster, Becca McCluster's mother. Donna these are Detectives Barns and Smith. We like to get together for some wine. It......helps us deal with.......you know."

The detectives say hi to Donna.

"They're working on the Abby Block case. They think there might be a connection between her case and our daughters' cases."

Donna said, "You detectives think that bitch Tammie Trolly was involved in my Becca's disappearance?"

Jackie said, "Yes we do."

Donna walks across the living room towards a window. She turns back around to everyone and starts to cry.

"The day that Becca came out to my husband Kevin and I........she was afraid about what we would think of her. I told her that........your father and I still love you and

149

always will.....no matter what. The stuff Tammie said to her..........*I'm surprised your parents still love you.....if they were **true** people of faith...they would beat the gay out of you.*"

She took a deep breath and continued.

"She's my only child. Without her I'm......I'm....."

Donna starts sobbing and Nina walks up to her and gives her a hug. Then.....both of them are sobbing in each other's shoulders. After a few minutes, Nina puts her head up. She walks over to a small picture of Alice in a black sweater with a pearl necklace and pearl earrings. She picks up the picture and takes it out of the frame. She then gives it to Jackie.

"Here......it's Alice's college graduation picture."

"Wait I have one too," says Donna reaching into her purse. It is a picture of Becca also in a black sweater with a pearl necklace and pearl earrings. She takes it out of her wallet and gives it to Heidi.

"This is Becca's college graduation picture. Detectives......find our girls....okay?"

Heidi and Jackie nod.

Ch. 36

The detectives get in their car and drive off. They sit in silence for a few minutes, then Heidi breaks it.

"I heard there's a park called Mellow Lane right around the corner from here. Wanna stop there and take a break?"

"Sounds good to me."

They get to the park, which is beautiful. It has a pond that's surrounded by a walking path and woods. There are several benches throughout the park. The two ladies sit on a bench and take in the view.

Jackie says, "A beautiful town......with possibly dark secrets. How cool is that shit?"

Heidi says, "Not cool if you're trying to nail a psycho bigoted bitch born with a silver spoon up her ass."

Both of them chuckle.

A few minutes later, they see Evan walking on the path. He looks terrible. His shirt is un-tucked, his hair is a mess, and his face is red and puffy streaming down with tears. He sits on the bench several yards away from the detectives. He puts his face in his hands and starts to cry......again.

Jackie says, "Is that......Evan?"

"Yeah........it is. He doesn't look so good."

"You're damn right about that."

"I'm gonna see what's going on."

"Okay."

Heidi gets up and walks over to Evan.

"Evan?"

He looks up, "Hey....you're that detective working on Abby's case. Uh......Detective Smith right?"

"Yes. You can call me Heidi."

He nods.

"Mind if I sit next to you?"

"No…….go ahead."

She sits down.

"Are you okay?"

Evan shakes his head and cries again.

Heidi puts a hand on his shoulder.

"What happened?"

"My mom was trying to set me up…..with a new girlfriend."

Heidi's eyes widen, "What?"

"Do you know what she *said* to me? She said that now since Abby's gone I needed to move on. Look at this as a second chance to date the *right woman*."

"My God…."

"I told her it wasn't right. She said that if I knew what was right I wouldn't date someone like Abby in the first place!"

Heidi puts her face in her hands and takes a deep breath.

"Heidi?"

She looks up at Evan.

"Do you have *any* idea what it's like for your parents to hate you because of who you decide to be with?"

"Yes……yes I do."

She takes a deep breath and continues.

"I married a black man. His name is Jordan and………I love him to the moon and back. I met him while I was having drinks with my cousin, Stacey at an outside bar in Bryant Park. He made the first move. Next thing I knew……a week after that…..we were walking around the same park holding hands on our first date. My friends adored him the second they met him and his family welcomed me with open arms. With the exception of Stacey, her parents, and her husband,.........my family pretty much distanced themselves from me. I knew that they wouldn't easily accept him right away. But as time went by and as my parents tried to set me up with other white guys who were marriage material........."

Tears start to well up in her eyes.

"I knew that they would never love Jordan........the way that his parents love me."

She cries for a moment. Evan briefly puts his hand on her shoulder.

Heidi takes another deep breath with tears still streaming down her face.

"I.........no longer speak with my parents. My daughter Sarah has......never met them and she *never* will. The day I told them that I will be marrying Jordan......I told them that there was nothing they could do to change my mind. They said.........well if that's how you feel.....then don't bother coming back. So......for Thanksgiving and......Christmas and.......other holidays.....we split our time between my in laws, Jackie's family, and Stacey, her husband, Colin, and her parents Aunt Stephanie and Uncle Steven. Aunt Stephanie is my mother's sister. The three of them...don't speak with my parents either. They're the *only* family on my side that Sarah has met and.......they love her soooo much and every time when I see her with Aunt Stephanie and Uncle Steven......I wish she had that relationship with my parents."

"I'm so sorry to hear that Heidi. That's.........terrible."

"Evan.......I need to tell you something. I know that what I'm about to say will be *very* difficult to hear. But.....you need to hear this. Okay?"

Evan nods.

"You're parents......are like my parents. They will *never* come around. They will *never* accept you and Abby being together. As heartbreaking as it is.......your parents might *never* speak to you again when you decide to marry her. Even though my parents and I are no longer on speaking terms.......I love my life the way it is right now....surrounded by people who *love* me and *care* about me and don't give a flying *fuck* who I married. Who love Jordan like he's family and who love Sarah like she's their own child."

Heidi takes a deep breath.

"Evan......why are you working for your parents' company?"

"Because every time when I was looking for another job-".

"They would ask you why are looking for one when you have your parents' company. Jackie told me what you told her."

Evan looks at Heidi.

"That's bullshit Evan and you know it."

"No it's not!"

Evan's eyes start to well up.

"With those tears you know it is. What's the *real* reason Evan? Tell me."

"I thought.......that if I worked for them.....and if they saw how good of a worker I was....they would be eventually be fine with me dating Abby because since I'm a good worker they would want me to be happy. But it didn't work......the plan didn't *fucking* work!"

Heidi reaches over and hugs Evan. He puts his head on her shoulder and starts to cry.

"It's okay Evan. It's okay."

After a few minutes, Evan lifts his head from Heidi's shoulder and rubs his forehead.

"You live in the city right?"

He nodded.

"How about Jackie and I take you to the train station okay?"

"Okay."

Ch. 37

Heidi, Jackie, and Evan arrive at the Broomville Train Station. The train to the city just arrives on the track when Evan gets out of the car.

Before he closes the door he says, "Thanks you two."

They both say, "You're welcome."

He closes the door and runs to the train. He gets on just before the doors close. The train leaves the station. The station is empty ad the sky is turning dark.

Heidi is about to drive off when someone suddenly appears at her window. Heidi and Jackie jump as they see Derek Hunting at their window. Heidi rolls down her window. He forms a smile on his face.

"Hi ladies!"

Heidi says, "Hi Mr. Hunting what brings you here? "

"I'm asking you two the same question."

"We're dropping off a friend to the train station."

"So Evan Pale.......Abby Block's boyfriend.......is your friend?"

"Mr. Hunting-"

"Get out of the car."

"Mr. Hunting-"

Derek pulls out a 9 millimeter and points it at them.

"I SAID GET OUT OF THE CAR!"

Heidi unlocks the doors and the two ladies get out of the car with their hands in the air.

Jackie says, "Mr. Hunting......we are just following our captain's orders."

Derek still has the gun pointing at them. He bobs his head towards his car.

"Oh you mean this guy?"

A woman gets outs of the car with Captain Tim.....whose arms are tied behind his back.

The woman says to him, "Don't do anything fucking stupid."

She walks over to Derek and stands next to him.

"Detectives meet my lovely wife, Debra!"

Debra says, "Hi ladies!"

Heidi and Jackie just stare at her.

Debra takes out her 9 millimeter and points a gun at the ladies.

"Take your guns out and put them on the ground."

She turns to Derek.

"I can't believe you forgot about that hon."

Derek forms an embarrassed look on his face.

Debra turns to look at Jackie and Heidi.

"I SAID TAKE YOUR GUNS OUT AND PUT THEM ON THE GROUND!"

Derek points the gun at Tim's head, "Do it or I'll blow his brains out!"

Heidi and Jackie slowly take their guns out of their holders and slowly put them on the ground.

Debra says, "Kick em' over here and keep your hands up!"

Heidi and Jackie do as they're told. Debra keeps the gun on the detectives.

Derek keeps the gun on Tim's head, "Now I want the three of ya to *back off the Abby Block case and any other case that is connected?* Do the three of ya understand me?"

The three of them do nothing.

Debra says, "Hey! Do you three fuckers understand him?!"

The three of them slowly nod.

Debra continues, "The next time we find out you three pull this shit again........not only are you screwed........your family's will be screwed too! AM I CLEAR?!"

The three of them nod.

Debra unties Derek's, hands, "Go with 'em."

Derek joins Jackie and Heidi. Derek and Debra keep their guns pointed at them. When Derek starts to drive off, Debra keeps her gun pointed at them. When they no longer see their car, Heidi walks over to the guns and picks them up. She puts hers in her holder. She gives the other gun to Jackie who does the same. The three of them are distraught.

Jackie begins to speak.

"Are you okay Captain?!"

Tim says, "Yeah.......I'll live. How about you two?"

Heidi says, "We're good."

"Ladies....we still need to stay on this case. It-"

Jackie says, "Captain.......I can't do this!"

She puts her hand on her head.

"Jackie-"

"They threatened my family Tim! I can't drag them through this shit!"

Heidi says, "I'm with her Tim! I can't bring my family into this."

"I thought you ladies wanted justice!"

Jackie says, "We want justice too Tim! But.........my family comes first! You got your wife, children, and grandchildren too! Do you wanna bring them into this shit?!"

Tim looks at Jackie and then shakes his head.

"I didn't think so."

Heidi says, "Tim......I really don't want to back off this case but........we have to."

Tim takes a deep breathe, "Okay. You're right ladies. Let's........go home."

Jackie and Heidi approach the car.

Jackie turns around, "Tim get in."

"Nah. I'll walk. Still Vo's is next to this town."

Heidi says, "Tim.....you just got kidnapped, had your hands tied behind your back, and almost got shot in the head. Get in the car."

Tim takes a deep breathe, "Okay."

He walks over and the three of them get into the car and drive off.

Ch. 38

Jackie and Heidi are sitting in a café having coffee in Hobleton, NJ, which is right across the Hudson River from NYC. They see Tim entering the café and he approaches them. He sits down and they greet each other. The waitress comes around.

"Hi sir. What would you like?"

"Coffee please."

"How about you ladies?"

"More coffee please."

"Okay. Comin' right up."

She walks away and Tim starts talking.

"Ladies......I'm so, so sorry for putting you through this."

Jackie says, "Tim....I mean Captain-"

"Eh...you two call me Tim. I get tired of hearing the word captain."

Jackie smiles briefly and continues, "Don't be sorry. You had no idea this was going to happen. And I'm sorry for going off on you yesterday."

Heidi says, "Me too Tim."

"Don't be sorry for that. You were right anyway."

The waitress comes back with the coffee. All of them say thanks.

Tim continues, "This case is important but..........putting our family's at risk..........it's not worth it."

Heidi says, "Well Jackie.......at least we had some time off."

She chuckles, "Of course."

All three of them smile.

The three of them pick up their coffee, clink their glasses together, and take a sip.

Ch. 39

Tammie Trolly

*Today's an exciting day! I'm sitting here at my vanity getting my face ready for the world to see: Foundation, a little bit of blush, some eye shadow (I **never** put any crazy colors on like blue or purple or red because the last thing I wanna do is look like a clown!), mascara, and lipstick. Jesus! Women back during my mom's prime looked classy and beautiful with their makeup on and their hair neatly done! These days with this damn feminist movement.....or whatever you wanna call it, women are walking around here looking like shit! They're walking out here without makeup on....and trust me.......they **need** it! Oh my God! Their faces look like someone just beat them up in their sleep! Their wrinkles and pores and spots.....you see **everything!** Things no one should have to see on a woman! Their bare lips look like someone took a cheese grater and rub them several times! And their hair! Oh my God! It looks like a damn bird's nest! With that sloppy bun look! Uh! It's like women have no pride in how they look anymore! It's a damn shame! No wonder men don't respect them in the workplace! I mean if you don't have enough respect for yourself to look nice when you're out in public.....how in the hell do you expect men to respect you?*

*Speaking of the workplace and this whole **thing** on women's leadership........it's **bullshit!** Oh yeah.....that women's initiative thing is just there for show! Just an FYI for you! I mean.....besides that bitch Danielle.....do you see any women on our family company's executive leadership team? Hell no! We hired Danielle because we had no choice but to have one woman on there you know for the diversity thing now that's a "trend." In my personal opinion......women shouldn't be in leadership roles of **any** kind. That's why I prefer to work for a man. They're so straight-forward. No catty bullshit! You see....men reward good-looking women like myself. Women well......if you're a good-looking female working for a woman....just be glad you've made it through the work day each day. If you're an attractive young woman like myself.......dealing with women everyday is like dealing with brown bears in the wilderness these days. That's why all of my doctors are men. The last woman doctor I saw was a complete bitch! I tried making small talk with her and unlike my male doctors who don't mind small talk at all.......she looked at me with suspicion........as if I was up to something!*

That's the problem with female leaders! They're sooooo damn paranoid about everything! They make everything so damn complicate! Knit pick about everything! I can completely understand why men don't want to work with women! Those types of women can be a pain in the ass! I mean who in the hell wants to hear your 'Oh I'm a woman hear me roar!' 'Look at me and notice me!' 'Respect me because I'm a woman!' 'I'm woman so I automatically should get an award for that!' 'I pushed out my child during hours and hours of labor so bow down to me!' 'I'm a woman leader so I get to treat others like shit because I'm above them!' Who in the fuck wants to deal with that prideful woman bullshit?!

I feel like this feminist movement has given women permission to be mean to everyone! 'Oh it's okay to be a bitch!' or 'Oh be empowered to tell others off!' or 'Oh you don't have to be nurturing all the time!' Uh! These **strong** *women come out looking for blood........especially from women like myself. Let me tell you something......women get nastier as they get older and men get nicer as they get older. Hello?! Have you seen an older woman running things? No! Why? Because who in the fuck wants to deal with a menopausal twat who hates any living thing that crosses her path? I personally think you should bring boxing gloves whenever you're dealing with women of a certain age! Because most likely....she'll find a reason to be a bitch to you! That's why I cringe whenever I see a woman running* **anything!**

What happened to the traditional values that this country is so desperately trying to hold on to? That a woman's place is to be nurturing and take care of her husband and children. That women held down the household while their husband's brought home the bacon. The men are here to lead and the women are here to support them! I see these **modern women** *working late; on their phones all the time with work related tasks, never spending time with their children. And you wonder why children act up these days: talking back to their teachers, being rude, raising hell! Children need their mothers to show them the way! That's a woman's job! Not working like a slave in corporate showing everyone that they can* **have it all** *and using their children as props instead of spending time raising them. That's not parenting.....that's just a selfish way of just getting attention and showing people how great you are at being a 'modern' woman! And guess who gets screwed at the end? The poor children of course!*

Oh I almost forgot to address this.......you're wondering why I'm working in the HR department at my family's company. Well it's because my father wants me to learn the family business. He doesn't want me to run the company when he passes away. My uncle's two sons will be doing that. But he wants me to learn the business because he believes that all the women need to be smart. I also went to college and graduate school full-time. But once I find myself a husband he and my mother want me to quit my job and become a full time wife and mother. And you know what.......I'm perfectly fine with that! In fact....I agree with that plan! After all......my womanly duties always come first! I'm currently dating this wonderful man James Wilt. His great-grandfather founded Wilt & Co. They're an investment banking company in New York City. James is a wonderful man who believes in traditional values! He wants me to be a housewife too! Since he'll be running the family business some day, I don't need to work! Why should I? We're the classy, traditional couple......except when we're between the sheets. My mother wanted me to be a virgin until the night of my wedding but.......James can't wait that long and......neither can I. That's why James has never cheated on me. I give him the prize several times a week and he **loves** *it every time! I swear if women gave men the prize more often...then their husbands wouldn't have to get the prize from another woman.*

Oh you're wondering why this is an exciting day today! Well……you'll find out soon!

Ch. 40

Tammie Trolly

Okay so I'm having the ladies from WMLS come over to my parents' beautiful mansion! Yes I still live with my parents because we believe that a woman stays with her parents until she's married. Anyway today's meeting will involve inducting Gabby Fry and Fiona Pipe you know, the girls that work in the HR department with me! Their parents also work for Charm Vault. Gabby's father is the Chief Information Officer and Fiona's father is the Chief Medical Officer. Both of their mothers are beautiful, dedicated housewives. The Fry's and the Pipe's are the epitome of the all-American family. My mother told me this morning that it was time for me to host these meetings and today will be my first time! Yay!

So let me give you a brief tour of my family mansion. We have a grand living room and kitchen with a large granite countertop island, 20 bedrooms each with their own bathroom and walk-in closet, my dad's office, and a reading room filled with books from top to bottom. We have a grand exercise room where Mom and I have our yoga instructor come over and teach us three days a week. Our extravagant backyard consists of a grand sized pool with a lovely waterfall and a slide that's on top of it. Next to it is a hot tub. We have two tennis courts for Dad when he invites the executive team over for gatherings and no....that does not include Danielle. We have a pool house with a full size living room, dining room, and kitchen. Upstairs, it has three bedrooms with a full size bathroom and a walk-in closet. Surrounding everything is a running path where I jog every morning to keep up my girlish figure! We also have a house down the Jersey Shore overlooking the ocean, one in the Hamptons, one in Martha's Vineyard, and we also have a condo in NYC on the top floor of the building with an incredible view of the skyline.

Ah! That's the doorbell! Let the fun begin!

―――――

Tammie, Gaby, Fiona, the three girls' mothers, and a group of white ladies of various ages are all seated in the Trolly's living room. They are wearing beautiful sundresses with heels on. Their faces are made up and their hair is done. Each of them have small wine glasses with the letters WMLS on them. There are several bottles of red wine on the coffee table where there are champagne flutes with the initials on them as well. Tammie opens the red wine bottles and pours the wine into everyone's small wine glass. Tammie rings a bell and begins to speak.

"Good Afternoon Ladies! Let's put our glasses down and bow our heads for prayer."

Everyone's head is down. Tammie continues speaking. She and everyone else form a cross with their head, chest, and shoulders as Tammie says, "In the name of the Father, the Son, and the Holy Spirit."

Everyone returns their hands to their lap. Tammie continues.

"God, we thank you for your guidance and support as we continue to maintain the greatness of this beautiful country of ours. We pray for Eric and Liz White as they sacrificed their freedom to promote the WMLS mission. May you watch over them and keep them safe. In Jesus Christ we name. Amen."

Everyone says Amen in unison. Tammie picks up her small wine glass.

"Everyone pick up your glasses and take in the blood of Jesus Christ; as he will protect you from the invasion of un-Americans and other evils in this world. Amen."

Everyone says Amen and drinks up.

Tammie picks up the WMLS binder, flips to a page, and continues.

"So our agenda today consists of a passage reading, then we will have our counseling session and then......the exciting part! The induction of our newest members, Fiona and Gaby!"

Everyone claps. Tammie takes out a piece of paper from the binder and continues.

"So today's passage is about the destruction of America."

She takes a deep breath.

"During the time when my beloved great-grandfather was alive and well, society was at it's finest in this country. It was the time when he started my family's company and started generating wealth for us......and I thank him everyday for his hard work. Don't forget.......it was around the time when your family started to generate wealth for all of you."

Everyone agrees in unison.

"That time, society was at it's finest because everyone knew their place and *stayed* there. The men were making money and the women were taking care of their families. Our people were running things and colored people were serving us. The gays stayed out of the way. *Everyone was in their place.*"

Everyone agrees in unison.

"Now.....women are trying to emasculate the men *everywhere* from telling their husbands that they *deserve* to work and neglect her kids at home, to being un-lady like when a man gives them advice by stating he's *mansplaining*. I mean....when a man speaks to you, you shut your mouth! See what this feminist movement is doing? It's permitting women to act out, to be selfish, to be unpleasant. It's permitting them to act like men and take charge of the money and power that the men should be doing, not the women. On top of that....they want to work into their late 50s and 60s...even 70s!"

They gasp.

"Now you ladies know what happens to our hormones as we get older. We get *hot flashes*! Also........and this is to my young ladies my age, if you think your mood swings are bad now during your time of the month.....wait until you are on menopause!"

An older woman named Heather Stare says, "Yes! I am so glad my husband is taking care of me and I get to stay home! I can save all the men in the workplace from dealing with my menopausal wrath!"

They briefly cheer and clap.

"Oh Tammie! I'm sorry for my input during your reading!"

"It's okay Mrs. Stare. You were right on the money with that one! Thank you for sharing your knowledge with us!"

Tammie puts her paper down and claps. Everyone follows suit. Then, Tammie picks up the paper and continues.

"You see back in the day, a woman knew to *never* defy a man. Those spiteful feminists called that being weak! Well you know what, I call it being well-behaved! The destruction of America right in front of our eyes!"

She shakes her head and everyone does the same.

"Now......colored people are starting to act out! They're *demanding* that they be treated with respect and like fellow citizens! Now ladies.....back in the day, niggers were classified as inferior. Today.....people don't even believe in that. Well you know what.....I still do! Niggers raising hell that they are treated terribly by police because they are black, that they are fired from their jobs because they are black, that they are followed around stores because they are black! Well the reason why they are treated this way is because they are *animals*! Animals that need to be dealt with a firm hand! And this is for all colored people...not just niggers! They are entering into *our restaurants, our neighborhoods, our schools, our companies, our hospitals, our politics, everywhere!* They are de-purifying our nation and it's terrible! It makes me sick! It makes me feel scared! Like our people will lose our place in society! On top of that.....you see these illegal aliens coming into our country! We got enough of colored people trying to colorfy our spaces! Now we gotta deal with these illegal aliens too?! Are you kidding me?! We can't have these colored people running our country! *Equalizing everyone!* Officially announcing that they are on the same level as our people! No way! Not in *my* country! The destruction of America right in front of our eyes!"

She shakes her head and everyone does the same. Then she continues.

"Now.......the gays! *They're coming out!* These *sinners!* And you know what's worse?! They are being *rewarded* for their sins! I mean......the medical community officially no longer deems homosexuality as a mental illness?! The legalization of *same-sex* marriages?! The legalization of *sin?!* Where were their parents when the devil led their gay children down the awful road of sin? Some parents did the right thing in terms of sending their children to the wonderful conversion therapy camps where they lead these sinners back on the path towards holy righteousness! Other parents sinned by *accepting* their sinful children because they *want their children to be happy.* Well guess what? There is no happiness in sinning! None of it! On top of that, you have these trans-sinners.....wanting to *choose* their gender. Well guess what? God chooses your gender. If you were born a boy you are a boy! If you were born a girl you are a girl! No exceptions! No mixing things up and destroying the categories that keeps the order of our nation! The destruction of America right in front of our eyes!"

She shakes her head and everyone does the same. Then she continues.

"The racial mixing of marriages and these sinful couples producing half bred children. The destruction of America right in front of our eyes!"

She shakes her head and everyone does the same. Then she continues.

"This MeToo movement or whatever it's called. The attack of men by unruly women who want to take over the duties that men so very deserve to have and using sexual assault allegations as a *tool!* The destruction of America right in front of our eyes!"

She shakes her head and everyone does the same. Then she continues.

"The tolerance of the sinful religions like the Jews with their greed, cheapness and extreme rudeness and the Muslims with their terrorist ways! The destruction of America right in front of our eyes!"

She shakes her head and everyone does the same. Then she continues.

"The Hispanics pushing our beloved English language aside and de-crowning it as our country's language. Condoning their people's illegal ways to get into this country and *destroy it* with their drugs lords and rapists! The destruction of America right in front of our eyes!"

She shakes her head and everyone does the same. Then she continues.

"The Asians making our people look like idiots compared to them with their people winning science fairs at our children's schools and outperforming our people in math and science! I mean can you *imagine* working for an Asian or seeing an Asian doctor? I don't think so! The destruction of America right in front of our eyes!"

She shakes her head and everyone does the same. Then she continues.

"The crazy Indians trying to *get their land back!* Our land back! The destruction of America right in front of our eyes!"

She shakes her head and everyone does the same. Then she continues.

"The bisexuals sleeping with both genders because they can't make up their minds! Slutty sinners they are!!"

*"The **destruction of America** right in front of our eyes!"*

The ladies cheer and clap for quite awhile. Tammie's mother, Beatrice, squeezes Tammie's arm and whispers into her ear.

"Excellent job honey!"

Tammie whispers back, "Thank you Mom!"

Tammie says, "Okay ladies. Our counseling session has now begun. Anything you would like to share with us?"

Heather says, "I do! I went to my doctor's office the other day and saw this woman doctor. She was nice but…….I wanted a male doctor but as the lady-like woman I am, I didn't say anything. After my exam, I saw the doctor who ran the practice and told him a little lie; that she called me a fat bitch and said that I was lucky to be married. He believed me of course….with my last name and all. As I left I saw him screaming at her and she was crying."

The ladies giggled and clapped.

Tammie says, "Thank you Mrs. Stare for pushing the mission of WMLS. Anyone else?"

Fiona says, "Tammie? Remember that nigger that worked in the IT department at work?"

"Yeah he was fired! I wondered what happened to him."

"Well..........I told my father that he tried to rape me......and that he took my underwear and put it in his drawer. My dad believed me. In addition to being fired, my dad also went to the police and pressed charges. Which was shocking because I made it all up. I put my underwear in his drawer. After all.....there were no cameras so......."

Fiona then smirked, "One less colored person in our world makes us better right?"

"Yes Fiona. Thank you for your courage for the greater good. Anyone else?"

Fiona's mom, Phoebe, gives her a kiss on the cheek and smiles.

A middle-aged woman named Stephanie Roster says, "I was at the jewelry store at the mall and I saw these faggots, a male couple, looking at things throughout the store. So I walked up to the store manager and lied by telling her that they called me the 'c' word. She believed me of course with my last name and all and told them to leave."

Everyone clapped.

"Thank you Mrs. Roster for upholding the WMLS mission. So anyone else want to share a story?"

The ladies shook their heads.

"Okay then! Let me get the champagne!"

Tammie leaves the room for a few seconds and returns with a few bottles of Champagne in an ice bucket. She puts it down and begins to speak.

"Gaby and Fiona please stand up and come over here."

They both stand up and walk over to Tammie. She give them a goody bag containing a sticker with WMLS on it (the same one Eric and Liz White had on their bulletin board in their basement), a coffee mug with those initials, and a white gold necklace with the initials in diamonds. Every woman there has the necklace on.........these two ladies put theirs on. Tammie continues.

"Ladies raise your right hand and repeat after me. Under God and the United States of America."

"Under God and the United States of America."

"I willingly take on the responsibility to uphold the White Man's Last Stand's mission."

"I willingly take on the responsibility to uphold the White Man's Last Stand's mission."

"With passion and dedication."

"With passion and dedication."

"Congratulations ladies! You two are *officially* WMLS women!"

Everyone cheers. Tammie and Beatrice open the champagne and pour it in everyone's glass.

Tammie then holds up her glass, "Great meeting ladies! Cheers!"

Everyone says cheers, drinks their champagne, and mingles.

Ch. 41

A young woman is driving to work the next morning and sees something weird moving on the side of the road in an office park.......where Charm Vault's corporate headquarters is. She doesn't work for Charm Vault. She pulls over and gets out of the car. She says to herself:

"Oh! Poor deer! Someone must have ran it over."

She gets a closer look at it. She starts screaming.

"Oh my God! Oh my God!"

The woman trembles as she dials 911.

The Still Vo Police Department are at the scene. The person is on the stretcher and being rolled into the ambulance. A black car pulls up and Jackie and Heidi get out. They approach the Captain.

Jackie says, "Tim......what's up?"

Tim responds, "I think you two ladies need to see for yourselves."

He gestures to the ambulance and the ladies head over to it.

As they get closer......they are shocked.

Jackie says, "Abby.........Abby oh my God?!"

Jackie takes Heidi's hand.

Abby looks like she went through the ringer. She is covered in blood, bruises, and lots of cuts. Her hair is matted with blood. Her face is all beaten up. Her eyes are struggling to stay open. She has a blanket over her.

Heidi asks, "Abby........what happened?!"

With a croaked whisper, Abby says, "I......escaped."

Then she slowly holds up her arm to point towards the direction of Charm Vault's offices.

Jackie asks, "You........were in the office?! Where?!"

Abby shakes her head, "No.......not in the office. In..........the dungeon in the woods by the parking lot. There's a tree...........with a red dot on it that's next..........to the parking lot. It turns out.........the rumor is true.........about a dungeon......being there."

A paramedic says, "Hey detectives. I'm sorry but we really need to get Ms. Block to the hospital."

Heidi asks, "Which one are you taking her too?"

"Taylor-Connor Medical Center."

"Okay."

The same policewoman who took Anna and Hector to the hospital at the crime scene of Eric and Liz White's house is there.

She says, "Ladies I'll ride with her."

Jackie says, "Thanks."

The officer gets in the ambulance with Abby and the paramedics and they ride off.

The detectives look at each other.

Heidi says, "We need to find that fucking tree."

Heidi, Jackie, Tim, and the other police officers surround the Charm Vault campus. They go into the woods. Heidi spots a tree with a red dot on it.

"Hey guys! I see the red button!"

She presses it and there is a huge vibration on the ground. A flat door slowly slides open and everyone makes way for it.

Heidi says, "What......the......fuck."

Finally..........the door stops. Heidi and Jackie head for the chamber first. Then everyone followed suit.

The hallways are dark and creepy. They walk for a few minutes and they see a large steel door. They see that the latch was opened from Abby escaping from..........whatever the fuck this is. They enter the room and..........the dungeon is huge. There are cages all over the place. Black people in the cages were in chains. They are about 50 of them. Their bodies were emaciated and bloody from what looks like whip marks on their backs. All of them are completely naked. Some of them were barely hanging on..........others were not. There was a cage that was opened. At the center of the room is a poll that is stained with blood. It's probably where they are tied up and whipped. There is a desk with a huge notebook on it. The detectives open it. It turns out to be a log. Each page shows a different place where people are being held captive. One page shows Eric and Liz White's names and shows who they were keeping captive, which were the undocumented immigrants. Other pages show someone else's name where they are detaining Asians, Jews, Muslims, Hispanics, and gays.

Everyone is staring at this with their jaws dropped. Finally.......Jackie says something.

"Oh.......my........fucking.........God."

She pauses for a few seconds and continues.

"Okay......um.......everyone get these people out of their cages. Find the locations of these dungeons in the book. There's gotta be addresses here somewhere."

As everyone unlocks the cages and tends to the victims, Jackie walks up to one of them. The woman inside the cage flinches a little.

"It's okay......it's okay......you're safe now. We are the police."

The woman stops flinching.

Jackie looks over her shoulder, "Hey! Can someone break this cage open?"

An officer comes with large pliers and breaks the lock. Jackie opens it and the woman slowly walks forward. A paramedic gives Jackie a blanket and she places it on the victim. The paramedics pull up a stretcher for her and she gets in it. They start to carry her upstairs to the outside and Jackie follows them.

Jackie takes her hand and asks gently, "Hey......what's your name ma'am?"

"Kelly."

"Okay Kelly........can you tell me who did this to you?"

Kelly works up just enough of energy to speak.

"The.......the Trolly family........Tammie.......Trolly........is the one.........who runs this. Her..........her parents.........Tom and Beatrice Trolly............came in here every now and then........to see.........how this was doing."

Kelly starts coughing.

"Did you see anyone else down here?"

"Besides new prisoners........no one else."

Jackie nods. The paramedics put her on a gurney and roll her away.

Heidi approaches Jackie, "We gotta find these other places."

The Trolly family approaches them.

Tom Trolly barks, "What the hell is going on here?! Get outta here now! You're distracting my employees from doing their damn work! They're looking out the damn window instead of making my company money! Now get the fuck outta here!"

Heidi and Jackie chuckle and make a smirk on their face.

"What the fuck is so funny?! Get outta here now!"

Heidi says, "Well nice to meet you too Tom Trolly."

She turns to Beatrice and Tammie.

"Oh and you two ladies must be Beatrice and Tammie Trolly."

Tom wags his finger, "Don't you *dare* speak to my family!"

"With a warrant for your arrest, that will be the least of your worries."

Jackie turns to Tammie and Beatrice.

"Oh and same thing goes for you two as well."

She signals the officers to come and arrest them. The officers cuff all three of them.

Tim walks over and says, "Make sure you state their rights. No short cuts. Got it?"

The officers nod and leave with the Trolly family.

Tim turns to the detectives, "I want you two to find these other locations."

Jackie says, "Got it Tim."

Jackie and Heidi walk away when they see Danielle. She has a look of absolute horror on her face as she sees frail........and dead bodies being pushed on stretchers.

The detectives look at her. Danielle looks back at them. She turns sharply and vomits on the ground. The detectives approach her.

Jackie says, "Danielle.........are you okay?"

Danielle turns to look at Jackie and wipe her mouth on her arm. She finally catches her breath.

"Detectives.......were all of those people.............*under* the company's grounds?"

Both of them nod.

"That family is *fucking sick! Sick!*"

Danielle sees the Trolly family being led out in handcuffs. She approaches Tom and walks beside him. Jackie and Heidi follow her.

"YOU FUCKING SKINHEAD BASTARD! YOU KNOW WHAT...... I QUIT! DID YOU FUCKING HEAR THAT?! I QUIT!"

She turns to Tammie.

"YOU FUCKING NEO-NAZI CUNT!! GO FUCK YOURSELF!!!!"

Jackie and Heidi take hold of her and the Trolly family keeps walking.

Heidi says, "Danielle.....Danielle......let them go. They're done as far as we're concerned.....okay?"

Danielle nods and then asks, "Wait.......was.......was Abby the one that was found here?!"

The detectives look at each other and then nod.

"Oh God no......oh no....."

Danielle faints on the ground.

Jackie says, "Hey! We need medical help over here!"

Paramedics come and assist Danielle.

Ch. 42

-Fiona Pipe and her parents, Bill and Phoebe Pipe are responsible for the captivity of gays. They were about 50 of them. Some of them were no longer breathing.

-Gabby Fry and her parents, Frank and Frannie Fry are responsible for the captivity of Hispanics. They were about 50 of them. Some of them were no longer breathing.

-Stephanie Roster and her husband, Ron Roster, are responsible for the captivity of Jews. They were about 50 of them. Some of them were no longer breathing.

-Heather Stare and her husband, Henry Stare, are responsible for the captivity of Muslims. They were about 50 of them. Some of them were no longer breathing.

The detectives and officers stopped at the last house........where the Asian prisoners are being held. Heidi knocks on the door. Derek Hunting.......the County Executive opens the door. His eyes start to widen.

Heidi says, "Mr. County Executive, we have a warrant to search your house."

"What hell is all of this shit?! Didn't I tell you two ladies to back off?!"

"And didn't I tell you that we have a warrant?"

Derek's eyes get dark and he gets into Heidi's face.

"*Don't get smart with me you little bitch!*"

"Or what Derek?"

Derek grabs her by the collar.

"You little-"

Jackie pulls out her gun and puts it on Derek's head.

"Let her go or I'll blow *your* brains out!"

Derek doesn't budge.

"I SAID LET HER GO! NOW!"

Derek lets go of Heidi.

"Now Derek, lead us to the basement."

Derek slowly turns around and walks ahead of them. Everyone else follows. They reach the basement. There is a steel door. Derek turns around and faces everyone.

Heidi says, "Open it."

Derek slowly opens the door and stands aside. The detectives and officers entered the room. There are about 50 Asians chained to the wall. The room looks similar to the room the undocumented immigrants were in at Eric and Liz White's basement. Some of them were barely breathing........some of them were not.

Heidi said, "Oh God........get paramedics in here now!"

She then turns to Derek and puts his hands behind his back.

"Derek Hunting you are under arrest for murder, kidnapping and assault on a police officer-"

"Assault on a police officer?!"

Heidi says, "Oh...so grabbing me by the collar on your front step escaped your memory all of the sudden?"

Derek shut his mouth and Heidi continues.

"You have the right to remain silent. Anything you say can and will be used against you in the court of law. You have the right to have an attorney. If you cannot afford one, one will be provided for you. Do you understand the rights I just stated to you?"

"Yes I do."

Heidi says, "Okay officers. Take him away."

Two officers take Derek by the arms and take him out of the room. All of the sudden......they hear a woman screaming at Derek. The detectives run out to see who it is. Debra is in Derek's face rambling and says this:

"Damn it Derek!!!! I told you to not let them in! Now we're both fucked! You know some of those yellows down there are *dead!*"

Jackie asks, "Debra honey..........so good to see you!"

Debra charges at Jackie.

"You pain in the ass little black bitch!"

Jackie punches her in the face. Debra falls on the floor covering her face with her hand.

"Ouch!"

Jackie squats down to meet at her eye level. She takes out her gun and puts it under Debra's chin. Debra's eyes start to widen in fear. Jackie clenches her teeth as she lays her out.

*"You do **not** threaten my family you little egotistical, skin head little twat. Do you understand me?"*

Debra just looks at her.

"ANSWER ME BITCH!!!"

Debra's bottom lip starts to quiver.

"Yes."

Heidi sees Jackie still holding the gun under Debra's chin.

"Jackie-"

"I'm not done!"

Heidi walks towards her.

"Jackie don't do it. That old scumbag bitch is not worth it."

Jackie looks up at Heidi. Debra still looks like she just pissed in her pants. Jackie pushes Debra, puts away her gun, and stands up. Debra slowly sits up and takes short, shallow breathes like she just ran a marathon for the first time. Jackie walks away. Heidi squats down and cuffs Debra. Heidi roughly pulls Debra up to her feet. The cuffs start digging into her skin.

"Ouch! The cuffs are-"

Heidi puts her mouth to her ear and clenches her teeth. Debra forms the same scared look on her face.

"After threatening my family that will be the least of your worries you old cunt. Now shut up!"

Heidi shoves her to several officers.

"Take her away."

The officers do so.

Ch. 43

Tim is in the middle of Heidi, and Jackie. They are staring at the evidence board in front of them. It contains the following hate speech that was in the basements where the victims were being held:

-Since Muslims killed Americans, let's kill the Muslims!

-Let's finish what Hitler started with the Jews!

-No gays! No way! Let's throw the gays away!

-Halt the Asian invasion before it halts us!

-End Hispanics before they end us with their excessive procreation!

-Hang niggers 'til their throats split! We don't need their stupid speech coming out of their big, ugly monkey lips!

..........and plenty more of the same thing.

There are White Man's Last Stand (WMLS) stickers *everywhere*. There are gruesome pictures of all the crime scenes.....filled with blood and frailness and.........pure evil.

Tim breaks the silence, "Well.......at least we know what WMLS stands for........"

Heidi and Jackie look at him.

Jackie says, "Yeah.....a eugenics crazy fuck shit. That's what this shit is."

Heidi says, "I was thinking Neo-Nazi fuckerade."

Tim continues, "I'm surprised none of them lawyered up."

Heidi says, "Because they know they're in deep shit."

Jackie says, "No. It's because they see this as them sacrificing themselves for the greater good.....in their twisted fucked up minds......just like Eric and Liz."

Tim says, "So.......who are we going after first?"

Heidi says, "Let's start with the Pipes, the Frys, the Rosters, and the Stares. Then.......we'll hound the County Exec and the Trollys. Sounds good Jackie?"

"Sounds good to me."

The Pipe Family

Jackie enters the room and sees Bill and Phoebe Pipe along with their daughter, Fiona at the table. Jackie begins speaking.

"Well, well, well! It's a family affair! I would've brought my family with me but.......that wouldn't be such a good idea considering what kind of folks you are. I mean homophobes like yourselves normally don't like black people....or gays for that matter. "

The three of them just stare at her with wide eyes.

"Yep......I'm a black lesbian and proud! Fortunately for me in the State of New Jersey.....you can't fire someone for being gay! Isn't that awesome?!"

They just stare at her again.

"So........you're being charged with murder and kidnapping."

Fiona says, "How can it be murder when Tammie told us that the only way to make this place holy is to exterminate people who are unfit for our society?"

Jackie glares at Fiona.

"What?"

"Tammie has a direct connection with God. She is leading us down the right path for us."

"If you're talking about the path that leads to prison....you're right about that. But the connection with God? Since when does God willingly give a connection to someone who lives in sin?"

"Tammie is not a sinner."

"Oh so.....killing innocent people by starving them 'til you can see their bones or beating them to a bloody pulp is not a sin?"

Fiona chuckles.

Jackie sits down across from the family and continues.

"Anyway we found Becca McCluster's body in your basement. So.....what happened to her?"

"I stabbed her about 30 times. Then....."

She leans forward and puts her elbows on the table. Her brow shifts down and her eyes go dark.

"I watched her bleed out to death. Seeing her suffer..........choke on her blood that was coming out of her mouth. It was the icing on the cake."

Fiona then forms a slow, chilling smile on her face.

Jackie hesitates for a few seconds, then says, "Why not kill her like you did with the others?"

Fiona's face turns red.

"Because I wanted that faggot to suffer the same way she made *me* suffer. *Always* getting ahead at the office. *Always* beating me at everything! I'm the *good* white person! A straight, white American; a *real* American! Why did she get more recognition than I did?!"

Jackie leans on the table and gets close to Fiona's face, "Because she *deserved it*! That's why! You don't get everything just by *showing up*! You have to *earn* it!"

Phoebe says, "Fiona stop talking."

Fiona turns to her.

"Shut up Mom!"

Then she turns back to Jackie and put that same, chilling look on her face.

"After all.......she knows *everything.*

Jackie chuckles, "Well....you're right about that Fiona. I have all the evidence.....including victims' statements, to lock all of you three up for a *very* long time. Have a nice life bastards!"

Jackie gets up from the table and leaves the room.

———

<u>The Fry Family</u>

Heidi enters the room and sees Frank and Frannie Fry along with their daughter, Gaby at the table. Heidi begins speaking.

"Wow, wow, wow! There's nothing like family crime is there? Anyway, let's get down to business. You're being charged with murder and kidnapping!"

Gaby says non-chalantly, "Okay...."

Frannie, says, "Gabby.....didn't you hear what the detective just said?!"

Gaby leans back in her chair and puts her feet on the table.

Heidi says, "*Get your feet off the table.*"

Gaby snickers and keeps her feet on the table. Heidi walks over and pushes her feet off the table. Gaby *almost* falls off her chair.

"Really bitch?!"

Heidi leans on the table and gets into her face.

"Didn't I just tell you to get your feet off the table.....bitch?"

Frannie says, "Gaby knock off the attitude!"

"Oh please Mom! She knows what we did!"

"You're right Gaby! I know *exactly* what *all* of you did. But I have one more question."

"Shoot."

Heidi sits across from them and continues.

"We found Alice Rodriguez's body in your basement where you kept the other victims."

"Yeah and..."

"What happened to her?"

182

She chuckles, "She died like everyone else in there!"

"I know *that* smart-ass. *How* did she die?"

She put a finger on her chin, "Well.......that was different than how the others died you know.........through starvation."

She takes her hand off her chin, puts her elbows on the table, and continues.

"I tied her down and slit her wrists until she bled out."

Heidi shakes her head, "Why....? She was your co-worker Gaby."

Gaby's brow shifts down and her eyes went dark, "That Spanish bitch.......please. She got on my last *fucking* nerve. Always beating me at *everything*. Taking on all of the major projects at work. That colored cunt should've been glad to even *have* a corporate job."

Heidi hesitates for a few seconds, then says, "And I'm glad that you're going away for a *very* long time."

Heidi gets up to leave.

Frannie says, "Wait Detective......that's it?"

Heidi turns around, "Um.......victims' statements, forensic evidence, your daughter's confession......yep....I got everything! Bye now!"

Heidi leaves the room.

———

Heidi sees Jackie and Tim in a room.....along with the Rosters, the Stares, and the County Exec himself and his wife. She enters the room.

"Jackie....Tim.....what is this?"

Tim says, "Oh Heidi! You came just in time! These fuckers are wondering if they're going to get off easy since the Trolly family runs this shit show!"

Jackie shakes her head.

Heidi chuckles, "You're kidding me Tim right?"

"Nope! I'm not kidding!"

Jackie points to the Rosters, "You kidnapped and tortured Jews to death."

Then she points at the Stares, "You kidnapped and tortured Muslims to death."

Then she points at the County Executive and his wife, "And you kidnapped and tortured Asians to death."

Then she throws her arms to the sides, "And......you *all* think you're not going to jail?! Are you Neo-Nazis fucking kidding me?!"

Jackie's arms fall to the side and turns to Tim, "You know what....I had enough of this shit for the day Tim. I'm outta here! I don't know about you Heidi."

"Right behind you Jackie. Let's get the fuck outta here!"

Tim says, "You two can go...I'll handle this."

The detectives leave.

Tim raises his arms, "So......why did all of you do this shit?!"

Then he lets his arms fall to the sides, "Enlighten me!"

Heather Stare says, "Like my husband and I were going to let those Muslim terrorists walks freely in *my* country!"

Stephanie Roster says, "Like my husband and I were going to let those greedy Jews get *every* sliver of our economy!"

Debra Hunting says, "Like my husband and I were going to let those Asians grab *all* of the powerful positions in *my* country!"

Tim is frozen in his stance, then he shakes his head, "Wow.......All of you are *evil.......sick bastards!*"

He turns to Derek.

"So Mr. County Executive! You have the balls to come and tell my team to lay off the Abby Block investigation but yet........you don't have the balls to talk yourself outta this shit.....and let your wife do it for you?!"

Tim chuckles and continues, "I guess those balls of yours are made outta glass!"

Derek charges at Tim and Tim flips him on the table in the center of the room. Tim gets into his ear.

"Don't even try it you bastard!"

Debra charges at Tim. Tim takes out his gun and points it at her.

"Debra......*don't do anything fucking stupid!*"

Debra stands still with a scared look on her face.

Tim puts his gun back into his holder, let's go of Derek, and opens the door. Several officers come in.

"Officers, get these fuckers outta here!"

Tim leaves as the officers deal with them. He sees Jackie and Heidi are looking through the one-way mirror at the Trolly family.

Tim approaches them, "So....how do you two wanna play this one?"

Jackie says, "How about all three of us go in on these fuckers."

Heidi says, "Sounds good to me."

Tim says, "Me too."

They enter the room. Tom Trolly looks like he just shitted in his pants. Beatrice and Tammie look as cool as cucumbers.

Tom says, "Ladies.....let.....me.....do the talking."

Beatrice snaps, "Oh please Tom! You look like you just saw a ghost and yet *you* decide to do the talking?!"

Tammie jumps in, "Uh....hello?! This was *my idea* to begin with! You two and the Frys, the Rosters, the Stares, the Pipes and the Huntings just carried it out! Well I carried my idea out with the niggers but other than that......I'm the orchestrator here!"

Tim says to Tammie, "I don't want you to *ever* say the "n" word again! Do you hear me?!"

Jackie says, "Tim it's okay! Let her say it as many times as she wants! I can take it!"

"Are you sure?"

"Positive!"

Jackie continues.

"So.......you're the one who kidnapped Abby Block!"

Tammie chuckles, "No I didn't!"

"Bullshit! We have her DNA on the whip along with every victim that was held in your dungeon and the poll where you tied her up to do so!"

"Yes! I did that to the others! But not Abby!"

"We are 100% sure that Abby's DNA is on the whip you used to whip her like you did to the others, and it's on the poll you tied her up to. We're waiting for the test to come back but.......we all know what the result of that is going to be. We know that you also tied the whip around their necks to choke them out......see if they came back to life. We also found marks on Abby's and the other victims' necks. DNA doesn't lie Tammie! But you do! We know you *hate* Abby! You can't stand her! Can you?!"

Tammie looks at Jackie.

Heidi says, "Answer the damn question!"

Tammie's brow drops and forms a chilling look on her face. She *slowly* tilts her head to the left.

"You did good Detective. Of course I hate that nigger bitch. You know.......the American office used to be a great place. *Real* Americans like myself had a place where we could *thrive*. People like me were in our place and people like Abby.......were in theirs. You see......people like Abby were cleaning up after us. Not being silly by going for jobs trying to get on the same level as us. Abby and her family are a threat to this country. Disrupting the American way of things. They make me fucking *sick!*"

Jackie shakes her head then continues, "Thanks for providing that useful information! Anyway.......look what I found?"

Jackie pulls out a sharp object in an evidence bag and puts it on the table. A look of shock forms Tammie's face.

She says, "Recognize this?"

"That's my........"

"Yes.....it's *your* envelope opener with *your* name engraved on it! We also found it in Abby's car! The one *you* stole and put deep in the woods where the dungeon is! The truck of the car has Abby's blood *all* over it! It has prints *all* over it! I'm sure these are your prints....especially when the test comes back to confirm it. We found *cuts* all over her arms, legs, and hands.....enough to shed lots of blood."

"I've......been looking for that for a while! I haven't used it for months! Someone must have taken it!"

Jackie chuckles, "Who a ghost?"

Tammie looks at her.

"Oh........and one more question. Why did you keep all of your victims at your family business' office? Why not do that at your house?"

Tammie sits back nonchalantly, "I don't want all of that filth in my house."

Jackie shakes her head, "You're a sick little bitch did you know that?"

Rick Triple, the Trolly family's attorney enters.

"I think you detectives asked enough of questions for the day!"

Jackie says, "Ahhh! You must be these skinheads' attorney! Well I got all I need....even a confession!"

"Not for the kidnapping of Abby Block!"

"No but....we do for the other victims in that dungeon!"

Rick turns to the Trolly's, "I told you three to not talk to *anyone*!"

Tammie sits back in her chair and sarcastically says, "Ooops!"

Rick shakes his head.

Jackie says, "Well.....you can walk with these shitheads down to central booking! Have fun in prison you three fuckers!"

Officers come in and cuff all three of the Trollys. Jackie, Heidi, and Tim leave the interrogation room. As Heidi approaches her desk, an officer walks up to her.

"Heidi.......the parents of Becca McCluster and Alice Rodriguez are here."

Heidi takes a deep breath and rubs the top of her forehead.

"Oh God. Okay.............um..............put them in separate rooms and......we'll take it from here."

"Will do."

"Thanks Bob."

Heidi slowly turns to Jackie with a nervous, concerned look on her face. Jackie is still standing at her desk.

"What's wrong?"

"Becca McCluster's and Alice Rodriguez's parents are here."

Jackie leans forward on the back of her chair and drops her head. She shakes her head.

"Damn........I hate doing this....."

"Me too. It never gets easier."

"Nope."

———

Heidi enters the room where Rafael and Nina Rodriguez are in. They are standing together holding hands.

Nina says, "Detective! We heard about the Trolly family being charged with murder. We were wondering if you found Alice! Did you?"

"Um.......Mr. and Mrs. Rodriguez........I think we should sit down for a second."

Rafael says, "Detective......why? Did you find her or not?"

"Mr. Rodriguez-"

"Did you find her?!"

Heidi starts to cry, "I'm very sorry Mr. and Mrs. Rodriguez............we found............Alice's body when we raided the Fry family's house. Gaby confessed to murdering her. I'm so sorry..........for your loss. I......really am."

Nina falls to the ground and starts wailing. Rafael is holding on to her and she starts hitting his chest, "Oh no! Oh no! No! No! No! No! No! Not my sweet Alice! Dear God! Not my daughter! Why did you take my Alice God?! WHY?! Ahhhhhhh!"

Nina buries her head in Rafael's shoulder and continues bawling.

Heidi comes over and kneels next to them on the floor. She rubs Nina's back.

Rafael asks, "Detective.......so Gaby Pipe murdered my daughter. Not........Tammie?"

Heidi nods.

"Why......why did she kill her? What did she say?"

"Because.........Alice got on her last nerve by getting ahead of her at work. Gaby said that that........"

"That what?"

"She said that colored cunt should've been glad to even have a corporate job."

"*Really?*"

Heidi nods.

He shakes his head and starts crying, "My daughter works *hard* to become the best woman she can be and *this* is what she gets! My daughter! My *only* child gets killed just for being herself. Just for being *good.* Just for being the smart woman she is!"

Rafael starts bawling now and Heidi puts a hand on his shoulder. Then she wraps her arms around the couple and mourns with them.

Jackie enters the room where Kevin and Donna McCluster are in. They are both standing holding hands.

Donna says, "Detective! Where's Becca! Where's my daughter? I heard you nailed the Trolly family and my husband and I thought you had an update on Becca."

"Mr. and Mrs. McCluster.........maybe we should sit down."

Kevin says, "Detective.....what happened to Becca?! Tell us!"

Jackie starts to cry, "I'm..........so, so sorry Mr. and Mrs. McCluster. We..............we found..............Becca's body when we raided the Pipe family's house. Fiona confessed to murdering her. I'm very...........very.............sorry for your loss."

Donna starts hyperventilating and crying, "This isn't..........happening!!! This isn't..............happening!!!! B-B-Becca.........i-i-is gone?! Is that what you're telling me?! My sweet Becca! My only child.........my daughter is gone?! Noooooooooo!"

Donna starts bawling. Kevin approaches her and she pushes him away. He approaches her again and she buries her head in his shoulders. Jackie approaches Donna and rubs her back.

Kevin says, "Detective...........why did Fiona kill her?"

"Because.........because Becca got ahead of Fiona at work. She said......."

"She said what?"

"Fiona said that she wanted that faggot to suffer the way she made her suffer."

"*What?* My........my daughter..........my daughter got *killed* for just being her. She.......she works her butt off to start her career.......and this is what she *gets?!*"

He shakes his head and starts to cry.

Jackie puts her arms around both of them.

Ch. 44

Abby is resting in her private room at Taylor-Connor Medical Center. She is hooked up to monitors. She is in a hospital gown and her wounds are covered in gauze. She has oxygen tubes in her nostrils.

Betty and Mark enter her room. Both of them start to cry.

Betty says, "ABBY! MY BABY!"

They run over to her.

Abby tries to sit up but it's too painful for her to do it all the way.

"Mom........Dad........it's you...."

She starts crying too.

The three of them form a group hug. After several minutes, they let go. Abby moans in pain.

Mark says, "Abby.....take it easy. You've been through a lot."

Mark's eyes well up.

"Excuse me."

He walks out of the room. Betty stays sitting on Abby's bed.

"Mom........what's wrong ....with Dad?"

"You're Dad is just.............worried about you dear."

"Tell him..........to come back..........in here.........Mom."

Betty forms a nervous look on her face.

"Mom....it's........okay."

Betty turns her head.

"Mark!"

Mark returns to Abby's room with his face wet. Abby gently pats a section on her bed.

"Come here.........Dad."

Mark slowly sits on the other side of Abby's bed. Abby grabs both of their hands. She starts tearing up.

"The two........of you..........have been...........incredible parents to me. Yes I've.......been through...........the ringer but...........I'm alive Mom and Dad. I'm........alive. You know........that it could've been.......a lot worse. But it's not..........you still.......have me. I still.........have you. Okay?"

They both nod.

"I........love you......very much."

They both say, "We love you too."

They form a group hug again.

Andrew, Allie, and Kate enter the room. Kate runs up to her and gives her a hug.

"Abby! I'm glad you're here!"

She starts crying.

"Hi.......Kate. I'm......glad too."

Andrew and Allie walk up.

Allie put her hand on top of hers, "I'm so glad you're home."

Evan enters, "Abby.....oh my God!"

He runs up to her and gives her a kiss on the lips.

"Evan......honey........so good.....to see you again."

He starts crying and puts his head on her stomach. Abby slowly puts her hand on his back.

"It's okay honey..........it's okay......"

Bill, Gayle, and Dave enter.

Gayle says, "Oh Abby......"

She turns to Betty. She gives her a hug and starts crying.

"Oh Betty! I'm.....so glad you have your daughter back."

"Me too Gayle......me too."

Dave walks over to Kate. He puts an arm around her and gives her a kiss on the forehead. He whispers, "I'm glad you got your BFF back."

"Me too honey."

Kate reaches up and kisses Dave on the lips.

Jackie and Heidi enter the room.

Jackie says, "Hey Abby. How are you feeling?"

"I've.......had.........better days."

Jackie nods and continues, "Of course. Umm......I know that this is difficult but......are you okay giving Heidi and I you're statement?"

Heidi says, "And if not......it's okay. We know you've been through a lot."

Betty says, "Detectives can this wait? I mean......I-"

Bill interjects, "Betty they're asking her this because sooner they get a statement from someone the better. It's better for Abby to give the detectives her statement because it's still fresh in her mind. Okay.......?"

She takes a deep breath, "Well.........okay."

Jackie says, "Can everyone give the three of us some time alone please?"

"But I want to stay with my daughter."

Abby says, "Mom.........it's okay. Let.......the detectives.........do their job. They're here to help me.........okay?"

"Are you sure?"

Abby nods.

"Okay........but if you need me I'll be *right* outside okay?"

Abby nods.

Reluctantly, Betty leaves the room along with the others.

Jackie and Heidi find chairs, pull them up to Abby's bedside, and take a seat.

Jackie begins, "So Abby........tell us what happened and......take your time."

Heidi says, "There's no rush."

"Well................I parked my car.........inside the garage. I got out......of the car when.......I felt like someone...........was stabbing me everywhere.......in my arms....my legs.......my hands. I saw ....lots of blood...........right next to my car. I was leaning against it ....when I look up.........and see.........Tammie holding a........sharp object that looked like an...........envelope opener. Then.......I blacked out. I woke up.........and............I found myself.......in the back........of my own car. It stopped......and I hear.....footsteps. Tammie opens the........truck door and pulls me out......I roll down the steps. I see this........steel door open. I enter........into this............dark room. There were cages........of black people..........who looked beaten..........starved........a few of them.......no longer breathing. She then.....tied me up.......to a poll......and started whipping my back. It felt..........like my back.......was on fire. The things she would say.............while she whipped me...........*Go fuck yourself nigger..............Die nigger die.............I should kill you now nigger.* Sometimes....she would......wrap the whip around..........my neck...........and pull. Then she would........put me back ....in the cage. Starve me like the others. I saw a............pile of dirt next to............my cage sometimes. I.......would eat that to.........survive. They barely fed us."

There is a few minutes of silence. Jackie and Heidi had tears that started welling up in their eyes. They look like they are about to vomit. Heidi breaks the silence.

"That's horrible.........Abby. I'm so very sorry you had to go through that. Can.........you tell us how you got out?"

"I saw.........some pliers next..........to my cage. I took them.........took all the strength............I had..........and broke the lock. I was able........to barely.........get outta there. Tammie was whipping............another victim. When she does whip them...........she's into it so much......that........she blocks...........everything out. One time........when I saw her.........whip someone else...........another victim kept screaming while she...........watched..........Tammie didn't flinch.........at all. I tried making it home but...........then..........I saw black........and passed out."

Jackie took a deep breath, "Abby......I'm glad that you are home. Thanks for giving us your statement."

Abby started crying, "I just........wish that.........I was able to......save the others."

Jackie and Heidi grab her hands and rub the top of them.

Jackie says, "Hey......don't.........think that. Don't. You had to think about getting *yourself* out of there."

Heidi says, "You...........couldn't save the others. Don't put that pressure on yourself. You did *nothing* wrong. Okay?"

Abby nods.

Jackie and Heidi lean in and give Abby a hug. Then they let go.

Jackie says, "Well.....we'll let you get some rest okay?"

Abby nods.

Jackie and Heidi leave the room.

Dr. Tiffany Gomez and Nurse Ann enter the room.

"Dr. Gomez.......Nurse Ann.......oh my God."

Abby tries to sit up but winces in pain.

Dr. Gomez sits on her bed and puts her hand on Abby's.

"Take it easy Abby. I'm glad you're......um."

Dr. Gomez starts to cry.

"I'm glad you're okay."

Ann sits on the other side and starts crying too.

"Me too."

"Thanks ladies......um Dr. Gomez?"

"Yes?"

"I'm......thinking about a career.........change. Remember.........when you suggested that I go............into Clinical Psychology? Well.........I was wondering if.......I could still.......talk to you............about that? Not now obviously but........"

"Oh of course Abby! I would *love* to talk to you about that. Plus.....we have several psychologist at the Sexual Assault Survivor Center here that would be more then happy to talk to you about it."

"You have............a center now? That's great."

Ann says, "It's named after her!"

"Mom?!"

"It......is?"

Tiffany nods.

"That's wonderful........congrats."

"Thank you. Well.......my mom and I will let you get some rest."

She puts her card on the table.

"When you feel better Abby, reach out to me so we can set up some time to meet. Okay?"

"Okay......will do. Thank........you."

"Of course. Feel better."

They leave the room.

Evan enters the room.

"Abby.........can I ask you something?"

"Sure....Evan."

Evan sits on the bed.

"Will.........you marry me?"

Abby eyes start to well up, "Of course............I will. Yes. Absolutely."

Evan starts crying too, "I'm sorry I forgot the ring. It's just when I found out you were here I..........."

"Evan....it's......okay. You popped.......the question. That's all............that matters.........okay?"

"Okay."

"Wait....how about......your parents?"

"Fuck them."

Abby smiles.

"I love you."

"I.........love you........too."

They both kiss on the lips.

She winced in pain again.

"Oh sorry Abby. Is everything okay?"

"Yeah.....it's just........I wish this pain.........would go away."

"It will sweetie. It will."

They continue to kiss.

———

Abby

I hope that cunt Tammie goes to prison for a long time. Because............this plan of mine was a pain in the ass......literally.

Ch. 45

Abby

Yes. You read that correctly. It was all part of my plan.

First...........I thought about taking pictures of her fucking with one of the pharmacists at Charm Vault and sending it to everyone at the company. He makes cocaine for her. Perks of working for a pharmaceutical company huh? Anyway.........I found that out by walking past there one night seeing her lying down completely naked on one of the lab tables with her legs up in the air and spread wide open. I saw the pharmacist completely naked on top of her seeing his butt cheeks squeezing in and out as he pushes himself inside her over and over again. After they both came, I saw him put cocaine on her breasts and sniff it up. She looked like she enjoyed that too with her head tilting back as he sucked her nipple afterwards. Then I saw her put cocaine on his dick and sniffing it up and then.........sucking it. He looked like he enjoyed it because his head was thrown back when she gave him a blow job. Frankly........it was a turn on watching them.........gives me potential ideas on what to do with Evan between the sheets. We don't do cocaine but.....well.....you get the picture.

Then......I thought about killing her. Kidnapping her, taking her to a place where no one could hear her scream, cutting her up into a million pieces with a machete while she's still alive, and burning what's left of that neo-Nazi cunt deep into the woods somewhere in Pennsylvania because doing that here in New Jersey would be too much of a risk. Killing her would be too much of a risk.

I got the inspiration from something I saw on the news. It was about a black woman who got acid thrown on her by a racist white woman while she was walking on the sidewalk somewhere in Pennsylvania. (Yeah, yeah. I mentioned Pennsylvania again. Get over it! That's not the point!) The acid burns were so bad that the victim died. The white woman got life in prison. Thank fucking God for that! However......shortly after the woman started serving her sentence......several inmates beat her the fuck up. That white bitch died a slow, painful death. They beat her up so badly, that she slowly choked on her own blood. Nice.

So......instead of me killing Tammie, I thought I'd frame her for doing a crime and let the inmates in prison do whatever the fuck they want to do to her. Stab her, beat her, shove a knife down her throat.....I don't give a fuck. I just want that bitch fucked.

So......the next step was to figure out how the fuck I was going to pull this off. First I thought about destroying one of my belongings at my apartment, staging a break in, and framing her for robbery. Then.......I thought about faking my own death and framing her for murder. But that's too much work. Plus why in the hell would I have my black ass live out in the Midwest in the middle of nowhere? After all.......most of those assholes out there don't even like people of color anyway so why would I even subject myself to that situation? By the way.......I wouldn't put my parents, Kate, and Evan through that either. So.....I came up with kidnapping.

*Now how to fake a kidnapping? Hmmmmm......that's a tough one. I thought I would have a struggle to figure out that one. But.......I got a break! Do you know how I found out about that dungeon? One night during my internship, I was leaving the office late; like 10pm late. Yes. I've been planning this for a **long** time. I saw this faint glow coming from the ground in the woods next to Charm Fault's office complex. Then I saw this sliding door wide open. Tammie was walking up to the ground from it. She left the door wide open. So while she was out, I poked my head in and checked it out. The steel door was also open. Oh my God! It was horrible! Black people in their cages suffering, the poll in the room covered with blood......it was awful. So I slipped out and got the fuck outta there. That moment it hit me! I would pretend to be one of her prisoners that got locked up in that dungeon!*

You're probably thinking 'Abby why didn't you report this to the police?' Well let me put it to you this way. If anyone told you that they found a dungeon full of people in cages........would you believe them? Yeah.....I didn't think so. 'Abby.....you could've taken a picture of it and showed it to the police.' Well do you think they would've believed me with a photo? No. Oh and by the way, I was afraid that someone would tip the Trolly family about me and........I really would've been fucked too. Plus.....I thought you would be smart enough to figure out why this was my plan to begin with. But...I guess not. I wanted that neo-Nazi bitch to suffer and I wanted to be the person to make her suffer!

So here is how I did it. First.....I had to make sure that the video cameras at my apartment complex were not working. So I cut the wires in the security room that controlled all of the cameras throughout the complex. How did I do that? Well the security guy that's on the night shift, he always takes a bathroom break at the exact same time every night.

So the night of my 'kidnapping,' I decided to put my plan into action. I picked that day because if I was kidnapped the day before I was scheduled to start the HR Program there, it would make Tammie look even worse for the crime. So I texted my mom back saying that I was home. Then.....I got out of the car.....left the front and trunk door open..........and stabbed myself with the envelope opener I stole from Tammie's desk at work. I stabbed my arms, legs, and hands just enough where I could still drive my car into the woods by the dungeon but enough where I could lose a certain amount of blood on the pavement. I covered my hands with gloves to make sure that my fingerprints didn't get on the opener. 'Abby how did you stab your hands?' Well............I took one glove off and stabbed that hand with the hand that still had the glove on. Then, I got rid of that glove, put another glove on the hand I just stabbed, and stabbed the other hand. Following me? Good! After I did that, I got in the trunk of my car and rolled back and forth in it several times to get my blood in there. Then..........I took some towels out of my bag and wrapped them around my legs, arms, and hands so the

199

driver's seat didn't get blood on it. I drove my car to the place near the dungeon. I placed the opener along with some of her hairs that I was able to pull out of her brush and planted them on the driver's seat and in the cup holder. Then I took the towels and gloves I used, went deeper into the woods, and burned them. Then I took my bag and went into the dungeon. I found that button, put another glove on my hand, and pressed it. I opened the steel door and then I went in and everyone in the cages was either sleeping or just out of it. So I was able to sneak in and grab the whip with my gloved hand Tammie uses on them and left. Then, I went to the next town over, which isn't such a nice town, and found a motel to stay at for some time. I was very careful to not eat anything. I had to make sure I looked starved so..........I ate dirt. Yeah....that was no fun. I was looking at the news and the only thing I saw about me was my school picture that was on the screen for three seconds and a 10 second blurb about me and that's it. Hmmm...no wonder this plan worked. Black girl gets abducted and nobody gives a fuck. Well......I'm not complaining because it helped me carry out my plan smoothly. After some time........I paid a homeless guy $500 in cash to take me to the back alley, put on a glove, and whip me over and over again to the point that my back bled. God that fucking hurt! I also paid him to choke me with it a few times. Anyway, after I was done, I put on another glove and returned to the dungeon. I placed the whip in there. Then I saw an empty cage that was locked....and found some pliers on the ground. So I took off my gloves, picked up the pliers, and broke the lock. Then I went inside the cage, put on a glove, took out the envelope opener and re-sliced my arms again, letting the blood drip in the cage. I took my glove off. Then I positioned the door in a way that looks like I escaped from inside it. I took my bloody arms, wrapped them around the poll and rubbed them against the poll where Tammie ties the prisoners up to whip them. Then I took the rope she uses, put it around my wrist and twisted them on my wrists until there were ligature marks on them. Then I took my bloody arm and got some blood on the rope. I dropped the rope on the floor. I pushed the button inside for the first time without a gloved hand and opened the steel door. Then I started running leaving the door to the dungeon open since it closes automatically within five minutes if you don't do anything with it. Then.........I just laid on the ground by the road for someone to find me.

I know! That was genius what I did! Haha!

Now in terms of the White Man's Last Stand cult that Tammie runs........I had no knowledge of that! Really I didn't! Now that shit took me for a loop! Well.....all of those who participated in this kidnapping shit are being charged with murder. Oh and you know what the good news is? In New Jersey, all murder is considered first-degree murder! I know! Awesome!

You know.....I'm so fucking tired of being the 'good' black person. The black person that dissociates themselves from being black to get their white co-workers to 'relax' in front of them; the black person who let's white people touch their hair; the black person who let's a white sales associate follow them around a store and walks out of the store as if nothing happened; the black person who smiles and nods when a white person says something bad about black people; the black person who stays silent as a white doctor

200

yells at them and demeans them for simply asking them a question; the black person who believes it's their mission and duty to do whatever it takes to make white people feel comfortable around them; even if it means they get screwed themselves.....or worse......killed.

Well let me tell you something about my black ass. I am not the kind of black person who will bend over backwards to make white people feel comfortable around me. Do you know why? Because one: I wasn't put on this Earth to do that and two: what's the point of me doing that if they will never change the way they see me anyway. As far as I'm concerned, it's a waste of time. Yes my parents are rich. Yes I am educated. Yes I'm smart. If that makes you uncomfortable.....then fuck off! Because I really don't give a flying fuck if you hate my black ass because of the three things I just mentioned. I am unapologetically **black** *and you'll just have to deal with it!*

Oh and I almost forgot to tell you about one more thing.........Jacka Rough didn't die from cancer.

I was scheduled to meet with one of the Human Resources Generalists at Taylor-Conner Medical Center to talk about my future working there since Dr. Gomez raved about me for helping out a rape victim. Anyway the HR clerk there went to the back to fetch one of them. Behind her I saw a huge filing cabinet. One of them was named terminated employees. I heard through the grapevine that the bitch was given the axe. So I went into the file and was able to find her name and address. Turns out she did have terminal breast cancer. Oh well....the bitch deserved it! Not only did she give rape victims a hard time but she also gave black patients a hard time too. So anyway this happened about a year ago. I saw her sleeping in her backyard with a cold drink on a small table next to her. She was sooooo out of it she didn't even notice that I was standing over her. I put on a glove and picked up the glass. It reeked of booze. Whew! What a strong drink she had. Well.......that was good for me because I took out a bottle of anti-freeze, poured it into her glass, and swished it around. Then I ran into one of the bushes and watched her. After about 20 minutes rolled by....she woke up. She turned right then left and rubbed her eyes. She picked up her glass and drank the rest of the liquid in it. Minutes afterward......she was choking.......until.......she took her last breath. When the coast was clear, I came outside of the bush, put on another glove, and checked her pulse with two fingers. That cunt was gone! Then.......I simply walked off. Let someone else find the bitch. After all, when they did find her........they assumed that she died from cancer. Not once did they ever think she was poisoned. After all........she looked like she would die any day now and she had no one close to her. Well.......that's what you get for being a racist, misogynist twat! Haha!

About Eight Months Later

Ch. 46

Abby and Kate are Survivor Navigators at the Dr. Gomez Sexual Assault Survivor Center at Taylor-Connor Medical Center. Their jobs consist of being a support system for survivors of sexual assault. They make sure that the survivors are doing well with their healing process such as being okay with the psychologists and social workers they're working with, sometimes going to their doctors' appointments with them, etc.

Abby is meeting with a survivor. She sat next to her and held both of her hands.

"So Bella, how is everything going?"

"Um….I don't know…….um…."

Bella starts crying. Abby gives her a hug.

"You know what….you are going to get through this. I know that healing seems far away from now. But…..you'll get there. Okay?"

Bella nods and they let go. Abby holds Bella's hands.

"Now let's just take several deep breaths. In through your nose…..out through your mouth."

They do this several times.

"Better?"

"Yeah."

Bella sees Abby's engagement ring.

"Nice ring."

Abby looks down at it and smiles.

"Oh thanks."

"When's the big day?"

"My fiancé and I haven't decided on that yet. But it will be sometime next fall."

"He's a very lucky guy."

Bella then looks down.

"I just hope a guy will still be able to love me after....you know......."

"Bella....what happened to you was not your fault. You did.......nothing wrong. You did nothing to deserve this. You will come out stronger from this and.........the right guy will be able to see that and adore that. *He* will be lucky to have you as his partner. Okay?"

Bella nods.

"Okay."

Abby notices that Bella is leaking clear discharge through her shirt, it looks like it's coming from her right breast.

"Um Bella.......are you okay?"

Bella looks down at her shirt.

"Oh my God! Oh my God! I'm so sorry Abby!"

"Bella don't apologize. It's okay. I'll get Dr. Gomez okay?"

Bella nods.

Abby gets up and pokes her head outside of the room. She sees Dr. Gomez and walks up to her.

"Hey Dr. Gomez."

"Oh hey Abby! How's my soon to be PsyD candidate in Counseling Psychology at Tumble Top University doing?"

Abby stays silent.

"Abby is everything okay?

"Um......I think Bella needs you for a moment."

"Of course."

Dr. Gomez follows Abby into the room and sees Bella. She notices her shirt right away. Bella has a scared look on her face.

"Dr. Gomez!"

"Hi Bella. How long have you been leaking discharge like this?"

"Um………I started leaking like this for about four weeks now."

"Did you see your OB/GYN about this?"

"Yes. I went to her as soon as this started but she…….looked at it and told me not to worry and the discharge will stop soon."

Tiffany's concerning look grew.

"Wait………..wait just one minute. She *told* you not to *worry* about it?"

"Yes."

Dr. Gomez sees a nurse pass by.

"Angela……can you get Dr. Allison Gardner in here? It's urgent."

"Of course. Right away."

"Thanks."

Bella's anxiety gets worse.

"Um……is everything okay?!"

Dr. Gomez takes Bella's hand.

"Bella……..I know this is scary for you right now. But………Dr. Gardner is an excellent doctor. You will be in *great* hands."

Bella turns to Abby, who grabs her other hand.

"Bella…….if Dr. Gomez says she's good. She *good*."

Bella nods.

"Okay."

Allison enters the room. She sits next to Bella and touches her shoulder.

"Hi Bella. I'm Dr. Allison Gardner. I'm a breast surgeon here. So…..what's been going on?"

Um Dr. Gardner.......can Dr. Gomez and Abby stay here?"

"Of course they can."

"Well....... my nipple started discharging this clear liquid like this for about four weeks now. At first it was a lump about several months ago; a relatively small lump; about the size of a pea. I went to my OB/GYN and she wanted to wait and see what happens and if I had any concerns that I should come back to her. Time went by and the lump got bigger to a size of a quarter. I went back to her and she still wasn't concerned and sent me home. Then time went by and the lump got bigger and my nipple started leaking this clear discharge. I went to her again and........she still didn't think it was a big deal and she told me not to worry and the discharge will stop soon. I told her that I was concerned about this since my mother died from breast cancer a few years ago at 50 years old and my sister died last year from breast cancer at 30 years old. I told her that I wanted a mammogram done for this. Then she just yelled at me saying that I was too young to worry about this and I was overreacting. I tried expressing my concerns again and she yelled at me saying that she is not having this discussion with me and she left the room."

Allison had a look of horror on her face.

"So your mother died from breast cancer a few years ago at the age of 50?"

"Yes."

"And your sister died a few years ago from breast cancer at the age of 30?"

"Yes

"I'm sorry to hear that."

"Thanks."

"May I take a look?"

"Yes."

Abby says, "I'll give you some privacy."

"Abby don't leave me! Please!"

She turns to Allison.

"It's okay Dr. Gardner. She can stay and she has my permission to know everything about this and so does Dr. Gomez."

Allison gently says, "Okay."

Abby says, "I'll get her a gown to put on."

Allison says, "Thanks."

Abby leaves and comes back with a hospital gown in a plastic bag. She opens the bag, takes out the gown, and gives it to Bella.

Allison says, "We'll step out of the room to give you some time to undress. Knock on the door when you're ready okay?"

"Okay."

Momentarily, Bella knocks on the door and the three ladies re-enter the room. Bella is in her gown and kept her pants on. She lays on the bed in the room opens the right side of her gown, which unveils a nipple leaking clear discharge. Allison puts gloves on and examines her breast. She feels a huge lump underneath her breast. Allison takes off her gloves.

"Okay Bella. You can sit up now."

Bella sits up

"So Bella……how old are you?"

"I'm 33 years old."

"Have you ever had a mammogram or an MRI done before?"

Bella shakes her head.

"No."

"Have you been referred to a genetic counselor before?"

Bella shakes her head.

"No."

Allison's concerning look on her face grows.

"Has *anyone* talked to you about your risk, any early screenings or anything like that?"

"No. I told my OB/GYN about this and she just flicked it off saying that she wasn't concerned about my family history at all. That black women develop breast at much lower rates than white women so I shouldn't be concerned about it."

Allison's jaw dropped and she was silent for a bit. She sits next to Bella on the bed. Then she takes a deep breath and holds her hand.

"Bella...........I am sorry that your OB/GYN didn't take your family's medical history seriously. The minute you told her what you just told me about your family history of breast cancer.........she should've been *on top* of that to a T. Your mother's and sister's deaths indicate that you have a strong family history of breast cancer. She should've recommended that you start breast cancer screening early and she should've referred you to meet with a genetic counselor about testing for genes that could increase your risk of developing breast cancer. The *fact* that she *punished* you for being concerned about your risk is *sickening.* After examining you, I recommend that you get this lump evaluated today and I also want you to meet with one of our genetic counselors today as well. Bella......I am *very* concerned about you right now and I want you to get this taken care of......okay?"

"Okay."

Bella starts crying. Allison puts an arm around her and Bella leans on her shoulder.

"It's okay Bella.......it's okay.......it's okay. Just let it out.......okay."

Tiffany sees Angela again.

"Angela...can you come here for a second?"

"Of course."

She enters the room.

Tiffany says, "Bella......Angela is going to take you to our Breast Center....okay?"

Bella nods.

"Okay."

Angela gently says, "Would you like to change back into your shirt or would you rather keep the gown on? It's up to you."

"Can I keep it on?"

"Of course you can dear."

Allison says, "I'll walk with you Bella okay?"

"Okay."

She turns to Abby.

"Abby......are you coming?"

Abby turns to Tiffany, who nods in approval.

"Of course."

Allison asks, "Oh Bella.......who is your OB/GYN?"

"Dr. Trick."

Abby forms a look of horror on her face.

Allison notices Abby.

"Abby.....is everything okay?"

Abby motions Tiffany and Allison to step outside for a second.

"I saw Dr. Trick one time for a check up. Let's just say........she has trouble with folks like myself. I made an appointment and she told me that I really don't need Pap Smears unless there's something wrong."

Tiffany says, "What?"

Allison says, "Are you *kidding* me?"

Abby shakes her head.

Kate approaches Abby. She whispers in her ear.

"Hey.....what's going on?"

"One of the survivors most likely has breast cancer."

"What?!"

"She got her symptoms checked out earlier by her OB/GYN and she just ignored her concerns......like they didn't matter."

Kate puts her hand on her mouth.

"Oh my God."

"Guess who's her OB/GYN?"

Kate processes the look on Abby's face.

"No.......fucking.....way. That Dr. Trick bitch?"

"She was just sexually assaulted and now.........she has to deal with this shit. This world is so fucked up."

"Tell me about it."

Ch. 47

Late at night, a group of white male and white female doctors gather on the ground floor of Beacon Health Ambulatory Care Center. They are all in their white coats mingling amongst themselves. Dr. Geraldine Jean approaches the front of the room. She rings a bell and the room becomes silent. Everyone turns to her.

"My fellow colleagues! Welcome to the first Medicine for a Better Society meeting! I'm glad that all of you could make it tonight!"

Everyone claps for a moment.

"Dr. Tess Trick, can you come up please?"

"Of course!"

Tess approaches Geraldine and stands next to her.

"So Tess and I have been noticing that this society of ours has been crumbling in front of our very eyes. We saw what the men and women of the White Man's Last Stand organization were doing. They had great intentions but...........unlike them.........we have the medical training to conduct the necessary cleansing of our *dirty* society that they didn't have. And do you know what else guys........we have the skills and abilities to get rid of these vermin and........make it look like a *medical accident*. As the Director of Radiology at the Beacon Health Breast Center, I've been putting my plan into action with every undesirable that comes into our center, including but not limiting to: niggers, homo-freaks, trans-freaks sadistic Asians, promiscuous Hispanics, terrorists Muslims, greedy, selfish Jews, *difficult* women. What I mean by difficult I mean women who don't act like the meek, polite ladies that they were biologically made to be; the women who come into our offices with their 'medical concerns' and......we all know that *those* women have the disorder of the worrying woman."

Geraldine rolls her eyes.

"Am I right?!"

The crowd cheers and then settles down.

Geraldine continues, "The mentally retarded, and the poor. I think I've covered everyone right?"

The crowd agrees and started cheering. Then...they settle down.

"Tess and I have come up with the conclusion that the vermin I just mentioned are destroying our society. Blacks who are nothing but filth and full of idiocy! So called 'strong' women who are diminishing our society's gender norms! Gays who are destroying the building blocks of what the American marriage is! Based on my professional opinion.....I think that the only way to make our society the best it can be is to cleanse it of these vermin!"

The crowd cheers for a moment, then settles down.

"Now......here is what I've been doing. As a radiologist at our Breast Center, whenever these undesirable women come to us, after they completed their scans, if I see a suspicious area in their breast........I tell them face-to-face that everything came back normal! And of course they believe me and never question me because I'm a doctor! Then I've noticed that these women's problems get worse. I've already had several of those vermin die from breast cancer due to my society saving work! My plan is working! How wonderful is that?!"

The crowd cheers again then settles down.

"Now Tess would you care to share your plan?"

"Of course Geraldine!"

Tess clears her throat.

"Well here is what I've been up to everyone! Whenever a patient that meets the qualifications that Geraldine just mentioned earlier.....if they come to me with a concern, I simply ignore it. I had a nigger patient named Bella come in with concerns about her nipple leaking clear discharge and she had a lump that had grown quite substantially in that same breast too. Her mother and sister died from breast cancer. I told her that her symptoms and her family history of breast cancer was not concerning to me.....even though us medical professionals know that her family history displays a strong family history of breast cancer and her symptoms are possible symptoms of breast cancer but........since she is a nigger, I ignored it instead. I'm sure she is well on her way to leaving us! Also since I deliver babies, if.....let's say....a nigger woman is complaining about severe chest pain after her pregnancy......I simply ignore them, tell them not to worry and let the heart attack take its course so she won't leave the hospital alive! I did that with several of my nigger patients last week and.......it worked!"

The crowd cheers again then settles down.

"So how do you like Geraldine's and I's plan to use our medical expertise for a better society?! Are all of you guys on board?!"

The crowd cheers in approval then settles down.

Geraldine says, "Okay everyone....let's do our salute! Now do as I do!"

Everyone stands up straight and holds their right arms up in a Nazi salute.

Geraldine continues, "Repeat after me! I pledge as a dedicated physician!"

"I pledge as a dedicated physician!"

"To use my gift of medical expertise to build a better society!"

"To use my gift of medical expertise to build a better society!"

"To take the oath seriously!"

"To take the oath seriously!"

"Unless the patient is part of an undesirable species!"

"Unless the patient is part of an undesirable species!"

"Okay ladies and gentlemen you can put your arms down now! If you have any questions on how to carry out your cleansing plan, feel free to come up here to speak with Tess and I! Plus if you don't have your cleansing plan in order right now, you have our information to come and meet with us at our offices to go over it with us! Okay?"

The crowd agrees.

"Good! Okay everyone! The meeting has concluded!"

The crowd cheers again. Tess and Geraldine clasp their hands together and take a bow. When they stand up straight again, they also cheer with the crowd.

Made in the USA
Middletown, DE
26 July 2024

57852612R00128